Cover by Jel - Dusted Design Brighton
Editor : Kristina Howell

I'd like to thank my son and my daughter for the inspiration to write this and for the initial idea that I now claim as my own.

These books are for my children, I hope they like them and I hope you do too.

Important: If you find this book somewhere and you've finished reading it or don't want to read it, please leave it somewhere for somebody else to find. Maybe not when it's raining, preferably a warm and dry place. If you have one of those little sealable bags, you know the ones with a ziplock you can put in the fridge, that would be perfect. If not I find leaving it on a bus, train or a park bench is perfect. Failing that just hand it to a friend, you don't even have to like them that much.

Yours Gratefully, Darius Z. Sutherland.

Chapter Zero

Hello there, how are you? Does it matter, do I care or am I just pretending? I thought I'd write one of the chapters, you know the ones, the twenty pages you have to read before the story actually begins. But this isn't like that, this is just a few boring words to help you understand.

This book, which I do try to keep short, was written in a lonely corner of a pub somewhere in the land at the end of a rainbow. I could tell you which pub, but that would be no fun now would it? As I sat week after week pondering what it would be like to be a writer, before I pondered no more. They say that most writers turn to the dreaded drink and I slowly began to understand why. It is a lonely and painful existence to write so that others can enjoy, all by your lonesome, watching the world go by.

I digress as I usually do and which you already may have previously found out, yet I still want to take you into my world, a world that doesn't really exist and it's also a place you wouldn't want to willingly visit. Imagine that, taking a trip around another persons mind; oh deary deary me.

So let's begin. To fully understand this story and to fully understand how I felt as I wrote these innumerable number of words, this is what you need to do first. I didn't follow this method the first time I began to place pen to the paper and

I'm not sure I would do it again, but never say never.

If you have access to a gramophone, a Hi Fi, CD player or Spotify, then I beg of you one thing. Listen to the music that I am sure you will find, it is called *Slip In Electro*. Listen to the music day after day, hour and minute after seconds and then only then will you understand the place I was in when I took Arty Grape and Mr Fox on their terrible journey. God Speed my friends, because if God does exist you will surely need him after this.

This Is Not A Happy Ending.

Chapter One

Once upon a time in a far away place, there was a beautiful princess who lived in a beautiful land. Everyone was blessed and everyone was happy. They lived in peace and harmony (you know like all the other stories you've read). But let me tell you children; it's all lies. They didn't live in peace and harmony, that's just what you've been told happens, there is nothing further from the truth. This story is *not* a happy story unless you reach the very end and even then I have been known to lie on more than one occasion.

In the West there was an evil king who sent his men to capture the princess from the other land, he wanted to keep her as a prisoner and a slave and do unspeakable evil to her until he got what he wanted. The evil king planned on marrying the princess, he planned to trick her into loving him, but he couldn't, for she was in love with another. The King's men were ordered to travel to the East and wait for the princess. They tracked her every move for days, followed her in and out of the village shops and when the time was more than perfect, they snatched her from the winding road that travelled back to her castle. The King's men felt proud that they had accomplished their task and they knew they would be rewarded in this life and the next. The princess screamed as they grabbed her horse, but nobody apart from the birds in the trees that surrounded them heard her screams, and even the birds had been frightened by her loud pitch squeals. Her screams slowly turned to whimpers as she realised her fate had already been sealed, she was doomed and not a single soul was coming to rescue her--Stop Stop Stop Stop Stooooooooop! I can't start a story like this, my children would never forgive me, in fact Arty Grape has positively told me that she would think it was an extremely rubbish way to start any story.

Oh hello. My name is something that changes all the time, depending on who I meet and who you are. I'll try not interrupt this story too much, but sometimes I just can't help myself. I like to talk you see, and sometimes you just can't stop me. This story is a true story and the names haven't been changed to protect the innocent. I am one of the children in these pages and I have the terrible task of re-living this tale so that all the children out there know the horrible and horrific truth. Stop reading now if you are easily scared. It may give you nightmares, you may wet the bed. I wouldn't advise reading it with the lights out, because you wouldn't be able to see; but not only that; the main reason is that you may never see the people coming that want to take you to the Homework Factory or if you'll ever come back. It is always advisable to look the person who is kidnapping you straight in the eyes. *Night night, sleep tight and don't let the bed bugs bite* I was always told when I was a child, but nobody told me about all the other things that lurk in the shadows of life. The things that wait for the children, the things that scare me, the horrible things you tell yourself not to think about. This story is about a small town called Eden, which as you know has always been a very strange. Towns are small and strange things always occur in these places.

The people in the town of Eden smiled but only on their faces, inside lay an undisturbed darkness that had become etched in their minds. There was an eeriness to Eden, something you couldn't quite put your finger on but you knew it was there. Everything was too perfect and the only way to go from perfect is down. Things were about to change for the people of the town and things may never return to normal ever again.

In the town of Eden sat a factory on one of the mountains that surrounded it. It had sat there for years and not a single person had given it a second thought. The factory had been abandoned a long time ago and its doors had always remained closed for as long as everyone could remember. The factory had become like a statue on the landscape, sitting dormant like a volcano, waiting to awake in a violent eruption of destruction.

In the town called Eden there was a little girl called Arty Grape and a little boy called Mr Fox. If you've read my previous ramblings, you will know all about these two wonderful creatures. You will remember that Arty Grape is a clever and curious young thing, you might even remember that she had long dark hair that reached to her knees, and her skin was like that of a Welsh Rose. You definitely wouldn't have forgotten that she liked to think and talk all the time, and there was no stopping her thinking and talking once she started.

Mr Fox was older than his sister, not in age mind you but in wisdom, he had very wise eyes that had a very different way of looking at the world. Mr Fox's hair was as wild and as long as he wanted it to be. They were brother and sister, they loved each other and they spent all their time together--That's enough from me for now. Let's start from where it all began shall we?

#

A fate worse than homework, is all the homework in the world.

#

On a very high hill at the edge of the town laid a gigantic factory. Black smoke poured from its chimney stacks and if you listened very closely you could hear the cries of children being carried by the wind, and on some days you could taste their tears in the rain. The strange thing about this factory was that nobody knew what its purpose was or at least none of the little boys and little girls knew. Those that had been there never spoke of it or ever told the perpetual tale of lies.

Whenever any child in the town of Eden asked their mums or their dads what it was, every little boy and every little girl in the town would be given a different answer.

That's where all the crisps come from.

That's where all the sweets come from.

That's where all the ice cream come from.

That's where all the jelly come from.

That's the place where everything begins.

#

In the town of Eden *everyone* is wonderful, there isn't a bad person to be found. If you were a bad person, you wouldn't want to live in the town called Eden because nice would be disgusting to you and you wouldn't be able to stand the stench. The mums and the dads and all the teachers that taught in the schools are wonderful, every single child that walked the streets are wonderful too. The town of Eden is a beautiful place to be, it is blessed with beautiful rose gardens that are dotted in every corner of the town. It had playful parks and ponds, where the ducks would swim gently in the crisp cool water. People said hello to each other in the streets, they stopped and they talked to each other, and they helped each other whenever help was needed.

There were two very clever and very special people in the town of Eden, their names were Arty Grape and Mr Fox. They were beautiful little things, with a beautiful way of looking at the world. A gift given to the young that is snatched prematurely away. Arty Grape and Mr Fox's mama and papa are also part of the lovely people that wandered the town. They played with them, they taught them and they disciplined them, teaching them how they thought they should behave along the way. Arty Grape's papa would say or do the strangest of things sometimes, but it didn't matter, he made them laugh. They all cared and respected each other. They loved each other and they spent as much time together as they could.

Sorry, me again, I can't lie to you anymore, I won't do it, I told myself I would tell this story and I would tell you the truth but I've lied, I did it this time to protect your fragile little soul. I hope even after I have told this little lie, you won't think different of me--As I was saying; everyone was nice in the town of Eden, except for one person. His name was Mr Jameson and he didn't seem to belong in the town. Mr Jameson taught most of the children at one of the schools and many of the children had heard many rumours about him, they had circulated the playground like a disease, and none of them were particularly nice to hear. Some children had heard horrific stories that had been passed down in time, through the ages, but none of them had actually seen these things with their own eyes. These rumours had been spread by all the older children that attended the same school as Arty Grape and Mr Fox, and these stories would always find the young impressionable children who's ears should not have to listen to such things. Let's talk about the story of Mr Jameson, it's not pleasant, so I am going to try and put it in the nicest of terms. If any child were naughty in his presence they would be punished and they would be punished severely. Mr Jameson would squeeze the head of a naughty child until their eyes popped out of their sockets a little, and then he would turn their eyes around so that the child would look into their own mind. That can't be pleasant! Arty Grape thought it was so ridiculous, it had to be true. She had heard how he smiled with such glee as he was squeezing a child's head between his hands. Nobody liked Mr Jameson and nobody liked being in his class. Every child behaved so politely in his presence because they feared what might happen to them.

'You boy!' What's the answer I am looking for?' he would shout.

Whoever his finger pointed at was in trouble if they didn't know the answer. So every child made sure that they knew everything that they could about what he was teaching. They studied hard every day for his class, they exhausted themselves keeping up with the work, until one day he never came returned to the school. The children sat in their class one day, they waited for him, but nobody came. The rumours began to circulate once again around the school. Some said that he was arrested by the police, some claimed he was thrown into the back of a police van with rabid dogs that were waiting to be fed, other people said a lot of different things, yet nobody knew what to believe or disbelieve.

Nobody knew what had happened to Mr Jameson, even though they weren't going to miss him they wondered where he had vanished to. He was gone but not forgotten, but the children had a lingering feeling that he would return one day in a different form.

Chapter Two

It was a Tuesday and it was a school day, in fact it wasn't any ordinary school day, it was the mother of all days; it was sports day. Arty Grape and Mr Fox had waited all year for this day. They couldn't wait to show off their athleticism to all the parents and all the other children, but most of all to their mama and papa. Their alarm clock sounded, it was 6:15am. They leapt out of bed and up the stairs; whoever got to the television first could decide what to watch. Their mama and papa would follow shortly and prepare breakfast. Arty Grape and Mr Fox had to get dressed first before they could watch the television, so they grabbed their uniform, frilly pants and cozy socks and they got dressed as quickly as they could. When they'd finished they could hear either their mama or papa walking up the stairs. They never knew which parent it was going to be until they heard the creak of the seventh stair. *It was papa* thought Mr Fox; he had come to give them breakfast and to make sure they were ready to go. 'Goooooooooood Mooooooorning.' papa sung.

'Good morning paps.' said Mr Fox.

'Good morning papa.' said Arty Grape.

'What would you like for breakfast today? Pancakes, cheerios, carrot and hummus, toast, fruit sal..?'

'Fruit salad please.' Arty Grape shouted enthusiastically.

'Shreddies with milk please.' shouted Mr Fox. Then they carried on watching the television. *The Amazing World of Gumball* was mesmerising them, it was a very funny show and even papa loved it. They laughed and they laughed until breakfast was served and they were summoned to the kitchen table.

'Breakfast you two!' Papa shouted.

'Can we eat in here?' Mr Fox shouted back. Papa looked at him and nodded his head.

'No.' he smiled.

'Aaaah. Please.' Mr Fox begged.

'No!' Papa said again. 'Come and sit on the table please.' There was no more discussion, Mr Fox knew that when papa said *no*, he meant <u>no</u>.

'Papa. Did you know some stars turn into black holes.' said Mr Fox.

'Your right, yes, they do turn into black holes. I think they implode not explode.' Papa mimed an implosion and explosion with his hands, he had always liked to talk with his hands, it was his favourite thing to do. 'I think they implode and then they turn into black holes. Do you know what a black hole is? I don't really, I've never seen one and I've never been to one but I've heard that once something goes into a black hole they can never get out again.'

'Because of the gravitational pull?' Arty Grape asked.

'Yes, that's right. I'm not sure but yes I think it's because of the gravitational pull. It's all in that space book Mr Fox bought.' They sat and they talked about space whilst they munched their breakfast down, Arty Grape was always first to finish but Mr Fox was the slowest eater in the world, he could take one hour to eat a couple of slices of toast..

'Okay. Get your bags together please, coats, bags, lets go, lets go lets go.' he ordered. Arty Grape and Mr Fox hurried around collecting what they needed before sitting back down to watch the television as Papa tidied up the mess breakfast had created.

'Okay. It's time to go now. Let's go, let's go, let's go.' Papa ordered once again, he had shouted the same thing for as long as he could remember but they never listened to him. He began hurrying them out of the door and out of the house. It was a glorious day, the sun was shining and the birds were still finishing their morning songs. They walked the short journey to school on foot, when the sun shone it was most pleasant, but when the snow had fallen and the cold wind blew the rain, it wasn't very nice at all. They walked past grand houses that mama wished to live in until they reached the recreation ground, the little bit of land given to the people of the town to enjoy for themselves. When they arrived at the rec Mr Fox always wanted to race his sister and his papa. Mr Fox still hadn't realised that the shortest distance between two points was a straight line, his papa would cut across the grass and he would stick to the path that ventured around, there was no way he could ever win his futile race.

The walking soon turned into a speed walk race, papa wiggled his bum and walked as fast as he could without running, Mr Fox on the other hand began to run, pretending he was just walking fast. 'That's cheating Fox. You can't do that. If you're going to run, then I'm going to run too.' Mr Fox giggled and he giggled as he tried to walk as fast as he could without running. Sometimes he would win the race, if his papa let him, but not today. 'I win.' papa gloated for a little, before shaking Mr Fox's hand.

'Well done for winning.' said Mr Fox.

'Good race.' replied papa.

They could see the school in the distance so it was time for their papa to leave them and send them on their way. He knelt down and gave them both a hug and a kiss.

'I Love you.' he said to each of them. 'Have a lovely day, be good and have fun.'

He had wanted them to be as independent as he could possible make them, so he let them walk the last part of the journey on their own, the part where anybody could snatch them, if they had been watching them closely enough.

'See you later smelly face, see you later puke head.' Papa shouted as he walked away, laughing to himself..

'See you later fart breath.' said Arty Grape

'See you later bogie hands.' said Mr Fox.

Arty Grape and Mr Fox had wonderful parents, they were so kind and they were so funny, they cared about them so much and it showed. That's what makes telling this true tale even harder. It's really sad what happened to the town of Eden and the people who lived there. It is a tale that its history wants to forget, but can't. It is a story that will live on in the children's children of Arty Grape and Mr Fox.

Chapter Three

Arty Grape and Mr Fox loved school. They played with their friends and they learned new things every day, they also had fun doing it. They loved all their teachers, both of them thought they were the most wonderful, kind and thoughtful people in the world, helping them through the day and through any struggles they faced, the very thing that teachers are there to do.

Arty Grape and Mr Fox walked towards the gates of the school, chatting to each other with every step that they took. Papa often wondered what they would talk about with each other after he had left them.

'I can't believe there's not a colour called burple.' said Arty Grape.

'Did papa trick you, I can't believe he tricked you.' laughed Mr Fox.

'I really thought there was a colour called burple. Papa told me when he was young there used to be a colour called burple. I've even written it a poem I made.'

'Ha ha, he's a joker,' said Mr Fox 'he's always told you he was a joker.'

'I bet nana's hair didn't turn white because she watched a really scary movie when she was young either.'

'No, that is true. Nana told me it was true.' said Mr Fox

with a serious look on his face, knowing it wasn't really true at all.

They carried their school bags on their shoulders and their heavy kit bags in the hands through the school gates and they made their way separately to each others's classrooms. Arty Grape bumped into one of her friends in the corridor and Mr Fox bumped into one of his too. 'Hello Luka.' said Mr Fox.

'Hi Fox. I can't wait until later. I can't wait for sports day.'

'Nor me, I can't wait to see who the fastest is. What do you think? Sky reckons she's faster than me. She might be, but we'll soon find out.'

'Sky is fast but I don't think she's faster than you, I'm faster than Sky and you're faster than me. I think you might be one of the fastest runners in the school or at least in our class anyways.'

'Really?' Mr Fox smiled to himself. He thought he might be one of the fastest, but not the actual fastest. They carried on walking and talking towards the cloakroom, they hung up their bags and they went into their colourful classroom where all the other wonderful children waited.

Arty Grape had met Issy B as she walked, like all children of her age Issy behaved in a delightfully grown up way, but unlike grown up's she didn't care about what she said. Issy just said it as it is, and as it was.

'Hi Arty. Are you looking forward to sports day?'

'Yeah, I can't wait. I'm looking forward to the hurdles and the sprint. What about you, what are you looking forward too?'

'I think the standing jump and the hurdles. I've been practicing the standing jump at home in the garden, I'm not allowed to do it in the house ever since I jumped on the cat.' laughed Issy B.

'I tried to jump over the table, and let me tell you that it didn't go very well.' giggled Arty Grape. They both giggled to each other as they walked to the classroom where Mr Clifton was there to greet them both with a warm handshake and smile.

'Morning Arty. Morning Issy. I hope you are well today?'

'Morning Mr Clifton.' they both responded in unison.

Mr Clifton stood at the entrance to the classroom until he had greeted all the children that came. Arty Grape hung up her bag, put her pencil case in her drawer and found her seat. Every delightful child sat in a different place each day so they could learn more about each other as they weeks and the years past. Today Arty Grape was sitting next to Mr Cousins. He was a bright young man, the cleverest in the class, he always looked sweaty and he would drool sometimes when he talked but that never seemed to bother Arty Grape like the other children. He was a mad kind of character but Arty Grape liked him, she always learnt something new from him every time they spoke. 'Did you know Arty that the sun is ninety-one million miles away from earth?'

'Did you know Arty sharks are made of cartilage.' These were just some of the things Mr Cousin would say to her.

There were a mixture of smelly boys and beautiful girls in Arty Grape's class and they all had their own unique personalities that hadn't been beaten out of them yet by hideous parents and horrible people. George F, Hanna Martin and Hanna Mitchel, Samuel, Arthur, Aggie, Molly, the list of names went on and on. It was their own world away from home. They were all best friends one day and they disliked each other the next. Hannah and Aggie always argued, they were two very headstrong young girls who liked their own way, and when they didn't get it--the 'holy moly' broke out.

'Right children, settle in and get your books out. I have to leave for a few hours, but the new substitute teacher Miss Potty will take over until I'm gone.' The children all giggled in unison, they thought it was such a funny name, they would never get used to it not being funny no matter how old they were, just like farts are always funny.

Mr Clifton rambled on about the explorer Marco Polo for a little while before he had to leave before Miss Potty entered to take his place. Miss Potty's name was no misnomer, she actually *was* a little bit potty, barking mad in fact. It's hard to explain the type of things Miss Potty did, she always seemed as if she wasn't quite right in her own head, like there was more than one person inside of her that battled to agree. She would wave her arms around all the time when she spoke, she would always lose her glasses and search the room for them creating a certain amount of chaos as she did, only to find them in her pocket. You would often come across Miss Potty talking to herself in the corridors, the dinner hall or wherever she might be; she didn't seem to mind and nobody else did either, it had just become a normal thing, it was Miss Potty after all.

'Okay children. Its sports day today, I can see you're looking all sporty in your kit. In a moment I want you to follow me outside and we'll make our way to the field. We shall form a single line, one by the side of each other. There will be no messing about, you will walk kindly and we shall behave ourselves. Anyone messing will be fed to the *thing* in the cupboard over there.' Miss Potty pointed to the corner behind the children. 'I'm sure none of you wish to be fed to the *thing*, do you?'

'Yes Miss Potty.' the children shouted.

'Okay then. Let's do it. Front tables first please.' Everyone shifted one by one from behind their tables to join the child in front of them, like good little children and obedient little sheep. Everything seemed to be working well, the children formed an orderly line and stood in their places, until George F became bored of waiting. George F decided to push his way to the front, barging each child to the side. It was unacceptable behaviour to Miss Potty. 'George, get in line now please. I won't have this silliness from you. Stop it at once. I am going to count to three.' Surprisingly he listened, but often he wouldn't, but the threat of *three* had made him snap out of his terrible behaviour and get in line with the rest of the children, he knew Miss Potty didn't mess around. Once he had settled Miss Potty guided them out of the classroom and they all marched slowly towards the field and waited for sports day to begin.

Mrs Keep blew the whistle to get everyone's attention; sports day had begun and the children mentally prepared themselves. They wanted to run, they wanted to jump, they wanted to have fun. Every child competed with each other in such beautiful ways, nothing mattered to them, they enjoyed every moment that engulfed them. They wanted to win but it didn't really matter, smiles beamed from their faces and laughter and chat filled the air. Arty Grape and Mr Fox sat patiently and waited for their turn. The fifty meter sprint was next for Mr Fox, and it was the hurdles for Arty Grape so they line themselves up on the starting line on different parts of the field. They stood besides another child from their year and breathed deeply in their heads and in their hearts, focusing on the task ahead, nothing but the white lines and the green grass on the track ahead mattered to them, they were ready for the task ahead; they heard nothing other than their own determined thoughts that coarse around their minds like it always had done.

'Go!' shouted Mr Ames.

'Go!' shouted Miss Bunn.

Arty Grape and Mr Fox dashed down their own paths that the wonky white lines had made on the painted grass. Nobody was going to beat them on this glorious day, they were focused on the finish line, they never even bother to glance in any direction other than forward behind, they concentrated on the right now and they did their very best. They ran and they ran until they crossed the finish line, their legs felt like they were creating fire for the first time, burning up the track beneath them and behind them. Arty Grape kept over each hurdle like a gazelle, she had no idea that she had left everyone else in her imaginary wake. Mr Fox stormed down the field, he was more focused than he had ever been on any other sports day or at any other time in his life. The determination in his face made him look like he was in pain, but he wasn't, he was in a zone, a world where nothing else mattered, no sounds could be heard and no other person existed. Each race ended and each race had been won by the other, but they were unaware of their victory until moments afterwards, as soon as they had discovered they had won a proud feeling filled their bodies.

Sports day soon drew to an end, all the events had either been won or lost, regardless of that silly fact every child received an ice cold lollipop to cool themselves down whilst they congratulated themselves. The sun was beating down upon everyones backs and they all wandered towards the trees in the shade to eat their delicious lunch provided by the school. Sports day had already become a distant memory, the children were now focused on their sandwiches and ice lollies, everyone was ready to enjoy the rest of the beautiful sunny day. Everything was perfect, and everyone was happy, the children giggled and the parents smiled.

This is always the part of a story where everything is about to go wrong for no other reason than it should.

Chapter Four

The end of the school day soon came, everyone was feeling weary from the day that had just passed, or at least the parents, the children were still buzzing with excitement, the lollipops were just hitting their brains centre and the fun was about to begin; but not the kind of fun that they had expected.

The children had had such a lovely time, they attended very little lessons and they learnt no pointless things, only fun had been achieved for the entirety of the day. They slurped at their lollies, savouring every last bit before they began to make their way home.

'Okay Artemis, it's time now, were going. Go and find Fox and tell him we're going too, and tell him to come over here.' Mama said in the sternest of her loveliest of voices.

'Okay mama.' Arty Grape ran off and searched the large field for her brother, asking anyone she knew or he did about his whereabouts. Eventually she found him sitting outside the cricket hut. 'Come on Fox, we're going now, mama's asked you to come.' Mr Fox knew he had to go, so he jumped up and said goodbye to his friends.

'I'll see you later Adam, I'll see you later Dino.' They all shouted goodbye to him and they all wished him well even though they didn't know what terrible things were heading their way, they were ignorant to the things that were to come.

'Let's go.' he said to his sister and spun around and danced his way towards her. Mr Fox often turned his movements into a little dance or a little spin here and there for his own amusement, it was second nature to him, but slightly strange sometimes for others to see. They made their way back to their parents, and collected whatever rubbish they had left on the school field along the way. *Always take your rubbish* they had been told and had never forgotten.

'Okay kids, lets go, lets get home, lets sit down on the sofa, lets chillax' said papa.

They walked home, down the beautiful roads aligned with large houses that hid swimming pools and olympic sized gardens, talking to each other as they moved.

'What's for dinner?' one of them asked.

'Can we watch TV when we get home?' asked the other.

Slowly they made their way towards the recreational ground and they all watched the sun set over the sea in the distance as they meandered through the recreational ground. Every day that they walked home from school the sky would reveal a different colour and nature would mesmerise them once again, never letting them forget how beautiful it could be. Everyone was tired and eager to get home, they each longed to sit on the sofa and to do absolutely nothing. If they could switch their brains off completely for a moment, they would. It isn't easy being bombarded with constant thoughts until sleep takes over you; only then do those thoughts turn into very different things.

'You were amazing today you two. I have never seen such speed and such determination.' said papa. 'Mr Fox you were like a bolt of lightning and Arty you were like some kind of super girl. I was amazed and I was so proud of you both.'

'Thanks papa.' said Mr Fox, with a big smile on his face and the stain of a red lolly on his lips.

'Thanks papa, it was so much fun and I think I did pretty good considering.' Arty Grape cheerfully said. 'Sky is so fast. Did you see her? For such a little thing, she can really run.'

'Considering what?' asked papa.

'I don't know, just considering.' she replied.

'Well how about you consider that consideration and let me know.' he replied, Arty Grape looked at him and told him he was weird without uttering a single word.

'Okay. I saw Sky, she's super-fast for such a little thing. She's determined, that's all I can say.'

'I beat her today and she reckons she is the fastest in our class.' said Mr Fox.

'Aaaaaaaaawwwwwesooooooooome!' papa sung. 'See, you had focus, determination and concentration, but most of all you had...'

'Fun!' they both shouted. Those words had always been the family mantra, drilled into them over and over again, so it would sink into their minds, brainwashed in a beautiful way--Fun is an easy thing to have when you have loving and caring parents; it's not so easy when their bodies have been taken over by an unknown evil, and they are no longer who they once were.

Slowly they walked home through the warm summer air, down the hills, across the roads and through the green fields. Finally they reached their home and exhaustedly walked up the steps that were never there, passing through the blue door that would always speak to them.

'Okay, pyjamas on, put your clothes in the wash, you know the drill' ordered papa.

'I'm soooooo tired,' said Mr Fox, 'my legs hurt.'

'Of course they hurt, you've been running around all day. The sooner you sort your stuff out, the sooner you can relax on the sofa.' said papa.

'Uuuuuuugh.' he groaned.

'What's for dinner?' asked Arty Grape grumpily, because she was tired.

'I have no idea. It's mama's turn to do dinner today. Mama what's for dinner?'

'What about liver, with fried onions and bacon bits. I know you two love that.' They didn't love it, they hated it but mama and papa always threatened to make it for them whenever they seemed ungrateful, they had decided a long time ago that they both despised ungrateful children; they would make them learn the hard way about the terrible world, which was coming and had arrived.

'I don't know yet, I'll have to see what I can make.' Arty Grape and Mr Fox went off and folded their clothes before they were told to do their homework. Chaos ensued, as it always did. Arty Grape and Mr Fox began to argue with each other, not because they were in an argument, merely because they were asked to do something they both despised.

When they finished their homework and tidying their room they were allowed to watch the television, when they had watched the television what felt like too long in the world of papa, they were told to go to the cupboard and find something to play with. Every thing that was meant to make them better people was always met by long and hard groan, until they accepted that was the way things were going to be.

'Why papa, Why do we have to tidy our bedroom?' questioned Mr Fox.

'I don't know, maybe because it's a mess, maybe because that's what children are supposed to do, maybe for no reason at all.'

'Well if its for no reason, maybe we don't have to do it.'

'Go tidy your room!' barked papa and the children jumped and ran towards their room. They knew he was being serious, they never liked the look on his face when he was as serious as serious could be. Their father could be as scary as a scarecrow when he wanted to be and they were as frightened as the crows could be.

'Dinner's ready everyone.' shouted mama, but nobody listened. Papa was engrossed in a new book, Arty Grape and Mr Fox were lost inside the different things they were doing. 'Dinner's ready' mama shouted again, it's going to get cold.' That was a lie, they were having salad for dinner and we all know a salad can't get cold. It took three more of their mama's cries before they listened and headed for the table to eat. She screamed with utter annoyance before they realised she meant business. They sat at the table and scoffed their food down their throats, eating in silence until the hunger pains in their stomachs faded away. 'Can we watch a movie after dinner papa?' asked Arty Grape. ', can we watch a scary movie? Can we watch...You know...That one with the alien you told us about?'

'You mean Alien?' laughed papa. 'No, you can't watch that just yet, but I'll try to find something suitably scary for you.'

'Aaaaaaw.' she moaned.

'Go sit down and I'll find a movie.'

Arty Grape and Mr Fox both ran and then jumped on the sofa. 'Who wants popcorn?' papa asked.

'Me, Me.' shouted Mr Fox. 'What movie are we watching?'

The Shining' whispered papa. 'We won't watch all of it, we'll just watch a little bit of the beginning.'

'Will it scare me, I don't want to watch a scary movie.' protested Arty Grape.

'What? You just asked me to watch Alien, thats a really scary movie.'

'I wanted to watch alien, but I don't want to watch this.'

'Tough luck Mrs Artemis, tough luck. Don't worry, it's not scary, you've seen The Women in Black, if you can watch that, you can see a little bit of this.' Papa fiddled with the television controls and tried to find the movie. 'If it gets too scary then I'll turn it off. I don't want what happened to Tommy Wallace to happen to you. I've told you about Tommy Wallace haven't I?'

'No. What happened to Tommy Wallace.' asked Mr Fox, immediately regretting his question.

'Well. Tommy Wallace lived next to me when I was eight years old. He was one of my best friends; we used to play together all the time. One day I went to his house to see if he wanted to come out to play. His mum answered the door and she told me he wouldn't be coming out, and she didn't know if he would ever come out again. You see, Tommy had decided to sneak into his dad's movie cupboard when his dad wasn't around. His dad loved scary movies you see, he was old enough to watch them, but Tommy wasn't. Tommy sat and he watched one of the movies, one of the scariest movies that his dad owned. He sat and watched it and within the first ten minutes he had become frozen with fear. He couldn't move or turn his eyes away, he was trapped watching all the horrible things the movie had to offer. Eventually his mind couldn't take it anymore. You see, your mind can only take so much terror before it terrorises itself. Tommy Wallace was frozen in fear; he is still frozen in fear until this very day. He's still alive but he's not there anymore, he's no longer with the world. He just sits in a chair staring blankly at whatever is in front of him, he can't move his arms, his legs or even his eyes. He can still hear, but some say he only hears the screams from the horror movie he watched on that terrible day-- Anyway, let's watch this movie shall we.' Arty Grape and Mr Fox didn't know whether that story was true or another elaborate lie that their father had dreamed up. They had a wonderful imagination and once it ran wild there was no stopping it. It didn't help that whenever their papa told one of these stories, he said it with such seriousness and such great belief, they didn't know he was lying until he told them he was. They would come to learn that they didn't really know him at all.

Everyone sat on the sofa and the movie began to play, Arty Grape become anxious as soon as the deep and unsettling music started play. The eyes of the children had been glued to the screen waiting for something terrible to happen but it never did, and that made things worse, the waiting that they had to endure. It's a bit like this story, nothing truly scary happens but it is the deep psychological scar the town of Eden leaves with in your soul that truly terrifies, how can such a beautiful place play host to absolute evil.

Thirty minutes had passed and Arty Grape was getting even more uncomfortable, she wriggled in her seat and at time hid behind her hands, Mr Fox just stared, he was mesmerised by a movie he wasn't old enough to watch just yet. 'Can we turn it off please papa, I don't like it.' she asked.

'You don't like it, what d'ya mean you don't like it? Nothing scary has happened yet.'

'I don't like it.'

'Okay, okay, we can turn it off. What about you Fox. What did you think abo....' Before he was able to finish his sentence, he was interrupted by the loud music that filled the air. Nobody knew where it was coming from but everyone could hear it. They all looked around themselves, desperately looking for its source. 'Where's that music coming from?' asked mama.

'No idea.' replied papa. 'Is it coming from outside, I'll go and see.' He walked out the living room and opened the front door to find where it was coming from. The music seemed to grow louder and louder the longer he stood outside, it started to hurt his ears and resonate through his mind and body. He watched all the other people from all the other houses walk into the street searching for the new sound that seemed to fill the whole town of Eden. They all looked around in confusions, up and down, left and right before one by one each of them began to spin in circles, until they were spinning in circles in unison. They kept spinning round and round without becoming dizzy and suddenly they all stopped and stared up at the mountain that surrounded the town of Eden. Mama ran into the street to see what was happening and almost immediately she began to spin in circles too before stopping to stare up at the mountains. All the children in all the houses witnessed this event through the windows in their houses. They washed and they waited hoping their parents would soon return to tell them everything was okay, but it wasn't. Arty Grape and Mr Fox stood in the window watching them watch the mountain, and then something changed. The people in the streets closed their eyes and began to sway in the absence of the wind, they had become lost in the music and then the music stopped. Each and every one of them turned around and walked back into their houses, somehow the music had changed their faces, they looked different to Arty Grape and Mr Fox when they came back inside, they had changed in a way that they couldn't explained, but they knew they were different. They closed the blue door behind them as they entered the house. Arty Grape and Mr Fox ran into the hallway to meet them. 'What was that music, where is it coming from? What just happened' yelled Arty Grape nervously.

'Sccccsssssssssssssssss.' They both hissed back at their children. They scowled and they grimaced, the evil that lay dormant in all human creatures showed itself for the first time in their eyes. Arty Grape and Mr Fox were filled with fear, something wasn't right, something was broken and they didn't know if it could ever be fixed. They watched their mama and papa walk away from them and climb the stairs and disappear into their bedroom

'What's going on?' asked Mr Fox.

'I don't know, this is really weird. I'm a bit freaked out.' They walked out the front of the house and into the street as cautiously as they could. All the people that were once there had gone, the street had become eerily empty; it wasn't just the street that felt empty, the air felt empty too. The music started to play again and Arty Grape and Mr Fox began to spin around in circles trying to see where it was coming from. Eventually they realised that it was coming from the factory on the hill, the factory that had been forgotten, but decided it now wanted to be heard.Waves of sound travelled through the air and entered their little minds.

Oh, jeepers creepers, where'd ya get those peepers?

Jeepers creepers, where'd ya get those eyes?

Oh, gosh all, git up, how'd they get so lit up?

Gosh all, git up, how'd they get that size?

This is the point, in this story of facts, that things begin to change. If you keep reading you might find yourself travelling with me to the darker side of your mind. You may find things that you don't want to discover in the tiny cracks of your psyche, the darker side of the moon is what we call it.

'It's coming from the factory Fox.' Arty Grape said.

'The factory. What factory?' asked Mr Fox.

'The factory on the hill'

'The factory on the hill. What factory on the hill?'

Like everyone else in the town of Eden, Mr Fox had forgotten about the factory on the hill. That is what the factory on the hill wanted you to do.

'You know. *The Factory!*' she said again, pointing at it sharply with her finger. When Mr Fox looked up upon its dark walls, it was like he was seeing it for the first time or remembering again.

'Really? It's coming from there.' Smoke bellowed out of the factory's large chimney stacks, it polluted every part of the air. They stared at it as it seemed to glow in the dim light that fell across the landscape. Arty Grape and Mr Fox didn't know what to do and they began to feel all alone for the very first time in their insignificant lives. They turned to go back in to their house, as they walked they could see their mama and papa in their bedroom window, they had a strange gaze on their faces as they stared at the factory on the hill that sat not he mountain. They stared and they stared and then they lowered the blinds. Mama and papa looked like demons who had been possessed by other demons, when they had scowled and hissed at them, their faces had changed, they were no longer the same people, they were no longer the loving mum and dad that Arty Grape and Mr Fox once had. They had become afraid of their own parents and they would soon discover that things had become the same in all the other houses across the town of Eden. The parents of each and every child had become infected by the music, it had cast a spell upon them that showed no sign of release.

Jeepers creepers, where did you get those peepers? Jeepers Creepers I'm coming for your eyes?

Chapter Five

The music emanated from the factory throughout the night, it played over and over stopping Arty Grape from getting a peaceful sleep, preventing her from escaping her strange and current reality. She lay awake counting the repetition of the works--*nine hundred and ninety nine times* she said to herself in her head. If she continued to count only insanity would follow she thought, so she decided to stop and to think about other things, like how rainbows formed and how amazing it always was to see the planet Venus in the dark winter sky. When the music finally released her from its grip, and she finally drifted into sleep, the music would continue to haunt her through all of her dreams. Mr Fox didn't seem to have trouble falling asleep, he had always loved his bed and he would always fall asleep as soon as his head rested on the pillow, today was no different from any other day.

The morning soon arrived, Arty Grape felt like she hadn't slept at all but she had managed to carve a few hours sleep out of the night. Upon awakening Arty Grape felt fine, it was as if nothing had happened and everything was as normal as could be, then a sinking feeling hit her, like a sucker punch to the gut. 'Are you awake Fox?' she whispered.

'Yeah. I'm awake.' Mr Fox had woken up before his sister, like he usually did, and he had laid there thinking to himself about the events from the night before.

'Do you remember what happened yesterday or have I just been dreaming?'

'No, I remember. I've been laying here thinking about them, I've been waiting for you to wake up!'

'What should we do?' she asked.

'I don't know, that's why I've been waiting for you to wake up. '

They hadn't seen their mama or papa since they'd disappeared into their bedroom the night before, and they hadn't heard them either. They knew something was wrong but they didn't dare ask what it was. Arty Grape checked the time on her newly purchased alarm clock. It was one hour until they had to go to school, so it was time to get up. They crept up the stairs and walked into the living room and closed the double doors. They sat on separate sofas and they both wondered why the music hadn't affected them and they wondered when it take them too. They were scared, but the only thing they could do was to carry on.

'What's the time Arty?' asked Mr Fox.

'I don't know.' she answered, whilst looking around the room trying to guess or find the time. 'It's eight o'clock.' she eventually answered, once she had found a watch that had been left on the mantle.

'What should we do?' asked Mr Fox himself another question.

'I don't know. I'm going to make some toast, do you want some?'

'Yes please.' he answered, it was the first time Arty Grape had made breakfast for him, he already felt like she was taking care of him. He followed his sister into the kitchen and watched her quietly make some toast. Every little sound they made felt one hundred times louder than it actually was, the opening and closing of the cupboard doors felt like nails being banged into the walls, the toast popped up from the belly of the toaster and to them it felt like a rocket being launched into space. Arty Grape buttered the toast gently but even that seemed like finger nails being dragged across a chalk board. Mr Fox went to the fridge to pour himself a glass of milk, but the milk bottle was heavier than he had imagined and he poured a great deal of the milk on to the kitchen surface, which then dripped profusely onto the floor. 'Son of a beep beep beeeeeeeeeep.' He cursed, as he found a towel to wipe up the mess. Finally they sat down to eat their measly breakfast.

'Shall we go downstairs and knock on mama and papas door?' asked Arty Grape sheepishly.

'Are you serious?' Mr Fox replied.

'I'm serious, everything might be fine.' she said, trying to believe her own words as she said them. Mr Fox thought about what she had said for a moment before answering.

'Okay, but you go first, I'll follow you.'

'Why don't we do it together?'

'Okay, let's do it together then, but you knock and you can open the door.'

'Fine.' she grumpily replied..

They finished their breakfast as slowly as they could, not knowing what fate awaited them after they'd braved the stairs, and the journey to their mama and papas bedroom. They walked slower than they had ever walked before; they were in no rush to find out what was waiting for them behind the bedroom door. Once they had reached the bedroom door they both waited for the other to make the first move and open the door.

'Go on then, you open it.' Arty Grape demanded.

'I'm not doing it.' Mr Fox said adamantly.

'I made breakfast' said Arty Grape ', so you can open the door.'

'I don't care, I didn't ask you to make me breakfast. I'm not opening the door.'

'Fine, I'll do it then.' Arty Grape reached out and slowly turned the door knob, and then she slowly pushed the door open, neither of them knew what to expect, but they braced themselves for anything. As the door opened wider, she could see the bed and they could see their mama and papa weren't in it. It took a few moments before they realized where they were. They could see them standing by the window, standing as still as jelly that didn't wobble. They watched their mama and papa stare through the glass as if they were staring at a brick wall.--Their minds had been temporarily been taken over, they both seemed to exist in a place very much different to the place that normal people reside.

'Mama, papa, we're going to be late for school if we don't go now.' Arty Grape nervously said, but they didn't answer, they just continued to stare out of the window. 'Mama, papa!' Arty Grape said again, but still received no answer. Mr Fox thought he would try to get an answer from them.

'Mama, papa.' he said, before they slowly began to turn, papa began to turn first and them mama slowly turned seconds later. When they'd both fully turned around and faced their children, they stared without saying a single word. Their eyes looked like the eyes of a dead animal, their expressions were blank and they grinned insanely in their direction. There was nobody home; mama and papa were two sandwiches short of a picnic and many crumbs from a whole biscuit.

'Come here child.' said mama. Her insane smile had faded from her face and it had been replaced with a more sinister and disturbing look. 'Come here child.' she said again, holding out her hand. Mr Fox began to walk to his mother but immediately Arty Grape grabbed on to his arm and pulled him back. 'Stay here Fox.' she said, and Mr Foxstayed exactly where he was, the gentle touch of his sisters armwas enough to reassure him. They all stared at each other for moments more, Arty Grape and Mr Fox didn't know what to do and they dared not utter a word.

Papa turned to Arty Grape.

'Leave us.' he said

'Leave us.' mama said, and then they both turned back to the window and began staring through the glass again as if they were waiting for some kind of signal to tell them what to do.

Arty Grape and Mr Fox knew there and then that something strange was happening, they knew something strange had happened but they didn't want to believe it until that moment, they felt on their own for the very first time in their life and they didn't know if everything would ever be the same again. They walked backwards out of the bedroom and quietly closed the door as the left. Arty Grape didn't no longer recognized her mama and papa, all she knew was that they weren't the same people they were twenty four hours ago. They climbed down the stairs in silence and sat down in the kitchen.

'What's going on?' asked Mr Fox worryingly, he was freaked out and terrified. 'Who are they, where are they?

'I don't know Fox, let's just get out of here and go to school.'

'Do you know how to get to school?' wondered Mr Fox.

'I think I remember. Let's just go, and I'll figure it out.'

They reluctantly left the house and hesitated with every little step, they didn't know where they were going or what they would discover along the way, or if something else would discover them.

As they walked further and further from their house, the place they never thought they would see again, the streets began to fill with more and more children. Every child in the town of Eden had become a wandering spirit, lost, without direction. They continued to walk down the busy streets, bumping into other children as they travelled. An older boy from school that Arty Grape recognized walked in front of her and she quickened her step to catch up with him to ask him some questions. She patted him on the side of his shoulder to get his attention and he turned to look at her.

'Excuse me. Do you know what's going on?' she asked.

'Don't look at me' he said. ', I don't know. I'm just following everyone else.' *He is just following everybody* else she thought, just like everybody else is following everybody else.

Arty Grape stopped as many people in the street as she could, but every other person knew as much and as very little as she did, so Arty Grape decided to follow them too. The children all shared the same hopeless predicament of travelling the same way without a guide.

In the distance Mr Fox saw a shimmering light, the sun was reflecting off the silver reflectors of his best friends jacket.

'Skye.' he shouted, 'Skye.' he shouted again. Eventually Skye heard him and turned around to locate the voice shouting her name. She looked left, then right and then behind herself. 'Skye, wait there.' Mr Fox shouted again. He ran to her as fast as he could, weaving between all the other bodies in the street. Arty Grape followed her brother, sometimes she followed him and sometimes he followed her; all Arty Grape knew was she didn't want to be left alone and she didn't want to lose her brother.

'Do you know what's going in Skye?' panted Mr Fox when he finally reached her.

'I've no idea Fox. All I know is that something strange is happening. My mum and my dad weren't the same yesterday, they scared me and they had strange looks on their faces. I don't know what's going on.'

'Were they staring out of a window?' asked Arty Grape.

'Yeah. They stood standing and stared out of their bedroom window. I didn't say anything to them. I just left the house and walked to school. I didn't know what else to do'

'I wonder if there's school today?' questioned Skye.

'I've no idea, I wonderd that too.' said Mr Fox.

'Do you know how to get to School?' asked Skye.

'I think it's this way' Arty Grape replied, ', follow me, it's not too far.' They carried on walking, all hoping they were heading in the right direction, but they didn't know, every child followed each other, and every child had great hope that they would find what they were looking for.

Arty Grape and Mr Fox soon found themselves staring at the school gates in the distance. They could see the teachers standing and waiting for them like they usually did. The bell rang three times, again, as it usually did, and the children went to their classrooms-But that's the thing. When you think things are the same, they are often nothing what they appear to be.

Every child found their way to their classroom and Arty Grape made her way to hers. She would always look forward to sitting down in her chair and wai for whatever knowledge Miss Sweet would impart to her. Miss Sweet was her favorite teacher, she would always give Arty Grape a little wink as she entered the classroom, and she always had very kind words to say to her every time she saw her, but not today.

All the children sat in their places and got ready for Miss Sweet to take the register. The children hoped that everything would be as it always was, but it would never be the same again. Miss Sweet wasn't sweet any more, or ever again.

Chapter Six

The music kept playing through the air, it would weave its words into the tapestry of the frightening day and then it would stop, before it started again at a different time.

Oh, jeepers creepers, where'd ya get those peepers?
Jeepers creepers, where'd ya get those eyes?
Oh, gosh all, git up, how'd they get so lit up?
Gosh all, git up, how'd they get that size?

Smoke bellowed from the factory on the hill, and unbeknown to all the children, preparations were being made for the reluctant guests that would arrive soon, taking their places, never to leave.All the children in the town of Eden were unaffected by the strange music, this made Arty Grape curios, it puzzled her and she always liked a good puzzle. She knew that the music was responsible for whatever was happening to her parents, but she didn't know why it had only affected them and not her and her brother. Arty Grape knew there was some kind of evil behind the music, an evil with a master plan. If you read to the very end, I promise you I won't reveal what or who it is.

The factory on the hill had sat there for thousands upon thousands of years, it always had a different purpose throughout its history. Sometimes it was used for good and sometimes the bad. The people in the town of Eden had forgotten this with every generation that was born; it was as if it had been wiped from their tiny little minds. Its true identity is buried in my head and in my head alone. Even I am discovering new things out about the factory on the hill.

The factory possessed a magical quality, it would feed from the presence and the emotions of others. No matter what century the factory found itself in, it always found its purpose. I could tell you so many other things about it and what it became, and I will, I promise you, just not now.

Arty Grape and Mr Fox had been visitors of the factory before, but they didn't remember. Every time they leave its presence, they are never themselves again, they are different people, reincarnated in different dimensions, with altered minds.

Oh, jeepers creepers, where'd ya get those peepers?
Jeepers creepers, where'd ya get those eyes?
Oh, gosh all, git up, how'd they get so lit up?
Gosh all, git up, how'd they get that size?

In a few chapters more, Arty Grape will become another reluctant guest at the factory on the hill. If you continue, I just want to let you know that this story doesn't end in the way you probably want it to. I'm just warning you now, that way you can't say *I didn't tell you so.*

Chapter Seven

Miss Sweet entered the room, Arty Grape could sense that something wasn't quite right, something was different, something was very wrong. Miss Sweet walked behind her desk and sharply turned like a soldier to face the class. The children stopped chattering and turned towards her, the others hadn't noticed anything different about her just yet but Arty Grape noticed that Miss Sweet didn't greet the children with her soft warm voice, her face didn't light up the room like it usually did as she entered it. Miss Sweet stood and Miss Sweet stared without uttering a single word, but the stern look on her face said everything the children needed to know--Miss Sweet was no longer sweet.

She continued to wear a stern look on her face, but even that managed to look expressionless, like the lights were on but nobody was home. She stood there motionless as the clock on the wall kept ticking away, interrupting the silence with every second. All the children sat and wondered when Miss Sweet would speak. Tick Tick Tock went the clock until it struck nine.

'ASSEMBLY.' screamed Miss Sweet, startling the children as she did and forcefully pointing at the door. The children now realised that something was definitely wrong. The children soon realised that the music had infected their beloved teachers too, they had hoped to turn to them for the answers they needed, but now they were presented with more questions.

The children scurried from their chairs and out of the warm classroom into the corridors, outside every classroom stood a teacher watching them children closely and carefully as they made their way to the great hall. There was nothing *great* about the great hall, it was like being inside a dull grey box with tiny windows letting in puny amounts of light. It always seemed unexplainably colder inside the great hall than it was outside, and the children could always see their breath leaving their bodies as they exhaled. The children squeezed themselves into the large space and settled in their places like sardines squashed into a can. Mrs Keep, the headteacher, walked towards the platform and spoke to the children. *What wise words does he have for us today* Arty Grape thought, and then she realised that all his wise words were probably gone forever. Even Mrs Keep wasn't immune to the music that spewed out of the factory on the hill, even Mrs Keep was no longer herself.

'Right everyone. There are going to be some changes at this school from now on and every other school too. No more of this nice stuff, none of that sickly lovey dovey nonsense. Oooh Jessica that's such a lovely picture you've done, oooh Augustus isn't what you've made so amazing. It's not, it's puke, it's worthless, just like you are. You only have one value to us now, you are our commodities and you shall go through life serving us. From now on it's all going to be about the homework and anyone not doing their homework and anyone not doing what I say when I say it will suffer the consequences. There will be consequences mark my words.' Mrs Keep raised her arm above her shoulder and clenched her fist. He was silent as he paused for a moment before dropping it sharply back down to his waist. 'Starting now.'

she shouted. 'Anyone talking and anyone not handing in homework will face an unspeakable wrath.' Mrs Keep didn't speak another word, she stormed off abruptly and left the great hall. As soon as Mrs Keep had disappeared from sight, they were told to get out and return to class by her assistant Miss Morrison, who carried out all of her misguided deeds in his absence.

'Get out and go back to your classroom,' he barked. 'if you have homework to be handed in, then you had better hand it in.'

The rest of the teachers began herding the children like cattle out of the hall, they were all shoulder to shoulder, and they crushed each other as they were pushed through the exit. They were marched in unison back to their classrooms. Arty Grape caught the eye of one of her classmates, Jacob, as she was herded out of the hall; Jacob saw her and fought his way back through all the children to talk to her.

'Arty, Wha...' Before he could get to the end of all the syllables, Jacob was grabbed hard on each shoulder by two teachers and he was violently dragged away. Arty Grape could see the shock and terror in his eyes as he was pulled away from her, he was pulled so hard it felt like he was being dragged to hell. Jacob did the only thing he could and he screamed hard and loud. 'Help, Help, Help me, somebody help me.' All the children including Arty Grape and Mr Fox ignored his cries because they feared they would meet the same fate, so all the children watched as he was taken away and Jacob was never seen again.

The children returned to their classrooms and they all sat down at their desks. Arty Grape sat in her chair and waited for Miss Sweet to return. Everyone sat in silence, they were all too scared to talk, already they were conditioned to the fear that they may face if they did, like pavlov's dog, they waited patiently. Tick Tick Tock went the clock and then the sounds of Miss Sweet's footsteps interrupted the ticking of the clock, each of her steps echoed down the corridor until she appeared in the doorway, which filled the children with a sense of dread.

Miss Sweet walked into the classroom and began barking orders at the children. 'Right everyone! I want your homework handed in to me immediately. Leave it on the desk over there. I want neat organised piles. Now!' One by one the children marched to the front of the room and placed their homework on the desk, and then they returned to their chairs to sit in silence. They sat there not knowing what they were waiting for and then the bell rang, it had never rung before and it deafened the children, some of them had to cover their ears to shield themselves from the pain of the sound. Miss Sweet stood at the front of the classroom, she was unaffected by the noise and she waited patiently for the bell to stop before speaking. 'Follow me.' she ordered, and the children followed her without question. They were marched back to the great hall with all the other children from all the other parts of the school and then they were forced into it once again, and the doors were closed tightly behind them, leaving them with only their thoughts and horrible feelings. No child dared to speak, no child dared to whisper. Some of the children in different parts of the hall began to weep and to whimper but nothing could be done about it.

The children were kept locked away until the end of the school day and only then did the doors of the great hall open to release them. A rush of fresh air engulfed the room and the children felt like they could breathe again; they gulped as much of the new air down as fast as they could, hurting their throats with every gasp. 'Leave now and return tomorrow.' said Mrs Keep. The children remained still, they didn't know what to do, nobody wanted to be the first to move and nobody was in a rush to go home. 'Leave Now' Mrs Keep calmly said again, and before they knew it the children found themselves wandering the streets again, trying to find their way back to their loveless homes.

Chapter Eight

Arty Grape found herself wandering with all the other lost children. Each and every one of them didn't have a home any more or at least what a home should be. They didn't know what waited for them, with each turn of a corner Arty Grape got closer to her house. She had looked for brother as much as she could but she was unable to find him amongst the despair of the other children. *I hope he finds his way home* Arty Grape thought.

She continued to walk the streets, following the other children until she had to follow her own way. As she turned another corner she bumped into Jazz, she had been friends with Jazz for as long as she could remember, they had told each other secrets that nobody else knew, but today Jazz ignored Arty Grape, she walked with her eyes firmly fixed on the ground whilst she navigated around her. Arty Grape looked around herself and she realised that all the other children were walking with their heads pointing towards the floor. The looked beaten, they all looked liked they had already lost all hope.

Arty Grape continued to walk towards her home, she would walk down the long road of Goldstone Villas until she found her house amongst all the other houses that looked the same. She always knew which house was hers, it was the twenty second house from the start of the road, it was two doors down from a shop and it was the only house in the town of Eden that had the number zero fixed to the front of its door. Arty Grape slowly walked up the path, she would usually run into the arms of her mama or her papa every day; she would usually be so excited to be home but she was filled with dread, on this usually, glorious day. She approached the door, the number zero seemed to make a low frequency humming noise that she had never noticed before. She rummaged through her bag looking for her keys, and then she slowly and very carefully put the keys in the front door, quietly turning them so the door opened. Arty Grape had no idea what would be behind the door, it had become a barricade between her and the terror she might find beyond it. Vivid thoughts flashed into Arty Grape's mind, one of those thoughts was being greeted by her parents, standing in front of her, with strange looks on their faces, motionless, waiting for her to join them. 'Join us' they would whisper. 'Join us and we will show you the truth.' they said again together. *There was no truth* thought Arty Grape to herself and then she realised she was answering a question that didn't even exist.

Arty Grape pushed to door slowly open and there in front of her stood Mr Fox; he greeted her as she entered. 'Hi Arty,' he said 'are you okay?' he whispered. Mr Fox had been waiting in the hallway, he had been standing there for some-time patiently waiting for her to arrive whilst he watched the light outside fade away. He placed one finger firmly over his lips, Arty Grape knew that this was the *silence* gesture that she had come to learn. Mr Fox pointed into the kitchen with his other arm, keeping his finger tightly attached to his lip. Arty Grape crept passed him into the kitchen and Mr Fox followed her, he closed the door behind him with a deathly silence. They were shut in, it would be very hard to hear them now from downstairs, but they still felt they needed to be as quiet as they could be.'Shhhhhhhhhhh.' Mr Fox whispered. 'Talk quietly.'

'Okay. Where are mama and papa?' Arty Grape asked.

'They're still downstairs in bed. I crept down earlier and listened outside of their room.'

'What were they doing? Did you hear anything? Did you see anything?'

'I didn't see anything and I couldn't hear anything either. Everything was quiet.'

'Quiet! You didn't hear a thing?'

'Well. There was this one thing but I couldn't be sure if they said it or not, it just sounded like it could have been.'

'What?'

'I thought I heard them say something like-- I can't wait until those children are taken away.'

'What?' Arty Grape whispered loudly..

'I can't wait until those horrible children are taken away. That's the only time I heard them say.'

'Something is very wrong Fox. I don't know what it is. Issy J doesn't know what it is, everyone I've been able to ask doesn't know what's going on and I now everybody doesn't want to speak.'

'I don't know either.' said Mr Fox.

They didn't know and they would never truly find out either, they would discover how the strange things were happening but they would never truly understand why. Just to let you know, I've decided to keep that to myself until my third book, when I realised what was happening it completely shocked me too, but then it became so obvious.

'I don't know what to do,' said Arty Grape. 'the only thing we can do is carry on as normal, we have to go to school like we usually do until we can figure out what's happening.' Arty Grape and Mr Fox would learn many lessons along their way and they would learn those lessons the hard and horrible way. Everybody finds out the hard and horrible way, and you will too I'm afraid, let's just hope it's not too horrific, let's pray together shall we, for all those things that might never happen.

'We'll have to make our own dinner tonight,' said Arty Grape. 'I don't know what to make; beans on toast will be the easiest thing to do. Hopefully I'll find a tin that has those sausages in them too.' They stumbled around the kitchen trying to find some pots and some pans. They located the beans and then the tin opener. They worked together to figure out how the cooker worked and how to open the tin.

'This knob must turn on this one.' Mr Fox said pointing to the back hob. 'Turn it on and see if it heats up.

'You turn it on!' barked Arty Grape. They had never had to use the cooker before, and they thought it might explode in their faces if they pushed or turned the only things that were meant to be turned.

Cooking their own dinner took longer than they thought it would take, they suddenly appreciated their parents, who were now lost to another world.

Arty Grape and Mr Fox finally sat down at the kitchen table to enjoyed their food triumph. The beans were cold and the toast wasn't toast at all, but they didn't care, they were starving and they stuffed every last bite into their mouths. Mama and papa still hadn't surfaced from down the stairs, there was no sign of them, they weren't coming to the rescue; their absence felt strange, but slowly and surely it became normal to them over the future days that would passed. Their parents and all the other parents in Eden were not themselves anymore, they're minds had been abducted, they could no longer see the wood for the trees.

Oh, jeepers creepers, where'd ya get those peepers?

Jeepers creepers, where'd ya get those eyes?
Oh, gosh all, git up, how'd they get so lit up?
Gosh all, git up, how'd they get that size?

Chapter Nine

Arty Grape and Mr Fox tidied their plates away, they were too afraid to leave a mess; it was then that they realised they had never been afraid before, they had been scared of things but never afraid and definitely never afraid of their loving parents. They never once worried that they would do terrible things to them. They had become afraid of their parents and they had become afraid of the things that hadn't even happened yet.

Arty Grape and Mr Fox sat down and watched a movie in the living room, the volume was a low as it could be; they played some games, they did whatever they could quietly to occupy themselves until they felt tired and needed to go to bed. Soon their eyes felt heavy and they knew sleep would follow soon. They got undressed and found their pyjamas in the basket in the cupboard, and they put on their pyjamas.

They both sat back on the sofa, they couldn't keep their eyes open, sleep had found them. Arty Grape's body jolted as she fought with the power of tiredness, and it was then that she realised she hadn't one her homework. *How could I have forgotten to do my homework?* she thought, as she jumped up from the sofa. How could she forget she thought again, her bag had been twice as heavy usual, its straps dug into her shoulders three times more than usual with every step, reminding her about all the white pages that needed to be completed. All the children had been warned by the head to do their homework, and they had been warned by all the teachers in all the classrooms too. Arty Grape became afraid of what fate might meet her if she didn't hand in her homework. She grabbed her rucksack and tore through it; she tried to find every piece of homework that had been given to her to complete. She flung books and papers over the room until everything was found. Arty Grape took a moment to breathe before she sat at the kitchen table to start the insurmountable task ahead of her, she began to panic more and more. 'What are you doing Arty?' asked Mr Fox. 'What's the matter?'

'I forgot about my homework, I need to get it done by tomorrow. Do you have any homework to do?' Somehow Mr Fox had completed all his homework or he hadn't finished lots of it.

'I have loads and I need to get it done by tomorrow or I don't know what's going to happen.'

I'll help you. I'll do some if I can.' They busied themselves with the homework; they made mistakes everywhere, but they didn't care, all that mattered was that Arty Grape could hand it in to her teachers when she was asked. One hour passed and then two, the night was about to turn into day, and they expected the sun to rise very soon. Mr Fox had tried so hard to stay awake, but he just couldn't do it any more. He laid his head down for what he thought would be a moment and fell instantly asleep, like somebody had given him a tranquilliser. Arty Grape continued working until she could continue no more; soon she was asleep, dreaming just like Mr Fox was.

The morning came without them realising. They had fallen asleep on top of all the papers, drool was dripping from their mouths and making the ink run on the sheets of paper. Arty

Grape was the first to rise, she opened her eyes and she was confused, for a moment she didn't realise where or who she was, she had just been put there by something unknown. The house was silent, there was still no sign of her mama or papa. They hadn't expected to fall asleep where they had worked, and there was nobody to remind them to wake up. Mr Fox turned to the clock on the wall. 'It's 7.30 Arty, we need to go!' If they hurried they wouldn't be late, so hurry they did. They jumped out of their chairs and ran in separate directions. Mr Fox went to get his uniform and get dressed. Arty Grape was desperate for the toilet, which couldn't wait. They hurried and they hurried, there wasn't time for breakfast, there wasn't time to breath, there was only time for the essential things that led them to school. They grabbed their bags from the floor and they ran out the door and there they were met with floods of children wandering the streets, children who were afraid to ask any questions. Arty Grape and Mr Fox joined the other children, they tried to blend in as best they could. It had been only one day since the terrible things had started to occur in the town of Eden but it was as if centuries of oppression had passed by the attitudes of the others. Mr Fox saw William, on the other side of the street; he too was following all the other children to school. 'William.' shouted Mr Fox. William stopped and turned towards him; he saw Mr Fox and he waited for him to catch up, waiting whilst all the other children barged past him. William was in Mr Fox's class, he was one of his good friends, Mr Fox always admired him because he could speak two languages even though he was still young.

'You okay William?' asked Mr Fox, he didn't seem to care if he was seen to be talking or not.

'I'm okay.' replied William cautiously.

'Strange things are happening.'

'Really strange things.'

Let me interrupt for a moment. I'm sorry about this but I did say I may do it from time to time, and I also said I'll try not to do it too much--I don't like describing the characters in my stories unless it's absolutely necessary. What they look like is sometimes unimportant to me. They assume the features of most folk so therefore I would like you to decide, I would like you to imagine. Imagine what they look like and imagine how they feel in their current and quite real predicament. Not all parents are nice remember, not all parents are like you or me, some of them do unspeakable things, and those things we shall not discuss here. There was no more playing red car, blue car, green car and pink car; those days were long gone.

'Do you know what's going on?' asked Mr Fox.

'No! I was hoping you or Arty did.' Mr Fox dropped his head towards the ground, he realised there were no answers and no question he could ask to settle his thoughts. They carried on walking and they followed the children that they recognised, like lambs to the slaughter, they walked to their eventual doom.

From above the children looked like tiny ants scurrying around but without any kind of order. Sky, Jacob, Hannah, Maisey and Luka joined Arty Grape and Mr Fox. Everyone was following Arty Grape and Arty Grape was following the NoWhereMan, she could see him in the distance, he actioned her to come his way.

Arty Grape arrived outside the domineering school gates, they appeared more daunting than they had a few days ago. As she walked over the threshold she felt a sudden sinking feeling in her stomach, it affected everything, even the tips of her eyes. The muscles in her face dropped and her legs momentarily became uncontrollable, she felt sick to her stomach and she immediately knew why. Arty Grape had forgotten her homework. She could see it in her mind, sitting there on the kitchen table, where she had left it. There was no turning back now. Miss Snell had already seen and fixed her gaze upon Arty Grape, it was as if she could smell Arty Grape's fear of the unknown. She was trapped in the tractor beam of Miss Snell's stare; she had no choice but to walk through the gates and to accept her fate. Miss Snell's eyes pierced her eyes as she walked; it was a cold deathly stare that would send shivers down anybody's spine, if they had one. Arty Grape walked past, what used to be one of her favourite teachers, and she hurried into the school. Miss Snell kept staring at her until she was out of staring sight. Arty Grape had a sinking feeling that she would see Miss Snell's stare again.

Chapter Ten

Mr Fox looked at his sister as they walked through the school doors, he could see the look on her face change . S h e looked worried, she looked scared. 'What's the matter?' asked Mr Fox, but his sister didn't answer him. 'Arty, what's the matter?' he asked again, her face looked even paler as the blood seemed to drain away from her rosy cheeks. She still didn't answer him. 'Arty, Arty.' cried Mr Fox. It was no use, Arty Grape was away with the fairies and there was nothing Mr Fox could do. They continued down the school corridors, watching all the children scurrying to their classes along the way. As he walked towards his classroom he wondered if his sister would be okay and then she broke her silence and spoke to him.

'Fox' she said, with a worrying look on her face ',I've forgotten my homework.' She looked at him and he looked at her, they both knew that no good could come from this, but there was nothing they could do now.

'Oh!' replied Mr Fox, immediately stopping on the spot. 'Where is it?'

'It's still on the table where I left it. I grabbed my bag like I usually do ever day, but I forgot to put my homework back in before we rushed out of the door.'

'Oh.' he said again. He didn't even ask what his sister was

going to do, because he knew it would be a futile question that not even the gods could answer.

'What am I going to do?'

'I don't know, tell them that you've done it, tell the you can go home lunchtime to get it, tell them anything.'

'Yes, I'll tell them that I've done it and I can get it at lunchtime, that's a good idea.' Arty Grape felt slightly relieved and Mr Fox felt good about calming her down and they carried until they reached the point where they went their separate ways.

'I'll see you later Fox, I'll wait at the gates for you after school, wait for me.'

'Okay. I'll see you there.' But Mr Fox wouldn't see her there, Mr Fox wouldn't see his sister for a very long time.

He carried on walking to his classroom, he would walk through parts of the school that were beautifully lit, with natural light streaming from the windows up high, other corridors were as dark castle dungeons. The corridors had emptied and he felt lonely as he walked the wooden boards alone, the doors to some classrooms were open and he peered in some of the rooms as he past, even though he never liked what he saw he kept looking through every open door that he could, torturing himself, hoping to see something that would put a smile on his face, but no smiles came. Each room was filled with children that looked like they didn't want to be there, each room was filled with a form of sadness that lingered through the air. Mr Fox kept moving down the empty corridors, his classroom wasn't far away but before he got there he wanted to do something he would always do when nobody was there to see. He carefully looked around himself, double checking his surroundings before he broke into a little dance. He loved to dance and Mr Fox needed to feel happy again, he needed to forget the simple worries that he had, so he broke into a dance that nobody else would ever see. He moved his body in a way that flowed liked water, each movement transformed into the next, he slid, he spun he twisted all of his moves across the wooden floor. He didn't care about anything in the world when he danced. Mr Fox didn't know what was coming next, so he decided to enjoy the moments that had been given to him there and then. How could he predict his future he thought, how could he know what was about to happen in the next second or hours. He jumped onto the floor and performed one of his new breakdance moves that he had been practicing, he executed it with perfection, but there was nobody around to see-- Another time he thought to himself. He jumped back on to his feet and carried on dancing down the dark corridors, for his final move he ran and slid, bursting though through the double green doors at the end letting a tidal wave of light engulf him. He was outside and he could see his classroom, a little cabin built at the back of the school. He stopped dancing and he cautiously walked towards his class, he could he didn't know what to expect, he didn't know what he was going to see when he entered the same room he had entered many days and weeks before. All he heard was silence emanating from the room and he felt uneasy with every step, he wanted to turn around and run, but he had nowhere to go, so he opened the door to his classroom and peered inside. It was then that he realised that there was something wrong with the town called Eden, he had hoped it was a dream that he would wake up from or a situation that would rectify itself, but it wasn't and it wouldn't.

Chapter Eleven

Arty Grape was terrified for what her future held as she walked down the corridors of the school. Every portrait hanging on the wall looked down at her with their wicked faces and they laughed hard at her upcoming demise. The closer she came to her classroom, the bigger the sense of dread she felt, she knew she would be asked for the very thing she couldn't give. Arty Grape continued her slow and gloomy walk to her classroom, she hadn't heard her brother trying to talk to her as they walked together, she could only hear her own terrible thoughts. She eventually reached her classroom and said goodbye to her little brother, even after he left she didn't want to go in. She stopped for a moment and other children pushed past her, knocking her left and then right. Arty Grape hesitated for a few more moments before she entered, the children sitting down laughed and pointed at her, they immediately knew she had forgotten her homework--but really they didn't, because it was all in her mind.

Children hurryed to find their seats in a blind panic, they didn't talk amongst themselves like they usually did, they found their seats and sat as quiet as could be, if not quieter. Miss Isleworth walked into the classroom and slammed the door behind her for no reason, or for no reason the children could think of. Miss Isleworth had always been a strict teacher, but she was strict because she was kind and caring not out of spite.

'Right! Everyone, bring me your homework, leave it here.' she swiftly said, pointing at her desk with her fingers. 'Bring me your homework!' she shouted at the top of her voice and then smiled with disturbing glee. The children rushed to find their homework from their bags, then they rushed to the spot Miss IsleWorth had pointed to, forming an orderly queue as the went. The children placed their homework on the desk and then they sat back down again as quickly and as smoothly as they could. Miss Sweet worth walked up to the pile of pages stacked on her desk and immediately she knew that something wasn't quite right. Miss Sweet looked around the classroom. Arty Grape felt like Miss Sweet could see through all the other children to find the one person that didn't hand in their homework, it felt like Miss Sweet was looking directly for her. 'Artemis Grape!' she bellowed. 'Come here!' she shouted again, beckoning her with one of her long and creepy fingers. Without any hesitation Arty Grape found herself drawn to her, even though she wanted to be as far away from Miss Sweet as possible, Arty Grape found herself unable to resist her command. She stood up and walked to the front of the class, all the children looked at her, thanking god it wasn't them, they all stared and had the look of pity in their eyes. As Arty Grape walked she knocked over a pencil case on George's desk, pens and pencils rolled across the floor and broke the painful silence that she found herself in, she quickly scrambled to pick them all up whilst everyone sat and watched her struggle to find each and every pen.

'Leave them!' shouted Miss Sweet, shocking Arty Grape back into her painful reality. As she walked to the front of the class she thought of Jacob and she wondered where he had gone, and she wondered if she would be taken to the same place. As soon as she became within grabbing distance, Miss Sweet pulled her sharply towards her with two hands and looked directly into her eyes. 'Are you trying to trick me Arty Grape? Do you think I am a fool Arty Grape? If you think I am a fool, just say it, we can be honest here, there will be no repercussions for your honesty.' Miss Sweet continued to stare at Arty Grape, waiting for an answer that would inevitably be wrong. 'Where is your homework my dear, did you forget it, do you think you are too important to do it?' Arty Grape didn't answer. 'I will assume you don't have it, unless you tell me otherwise, because I am not looking for any excuses from you, excuses will not be tolerated anymore.' Miss Sweet waited for an answer but Arty Grape remained silent, she had lost all of her words, they had been eaten by the fear inside. Miss Sweet violently pulled Arty Grape out of the room and in to the corridor. The children sat in horror at what they had just witnessed and from that day forth they pretended that Arty Grape had never disappeared, because it was easier to feel like she had never existed, rather than have been taken away.

Where had Arty Grape Gone? Is what the children dared never to ask.

Chapter Twelve

The end of the day approached and the children poured from the gates of the school into the empty streets, they dragged their broken body' until they found their way home again, where nothing was waiting for them. The children were emotionally drained, they had been worked hard in the classroom and they were expected to work hard when they returned home, they had nothing to look forward too anymore, apart from homework. As they walked their eyes faced the floor, their shoulders were hunched and their spirit was worn. Confusion haunted them and sadness filled their hearts, every day soon became the same as the one that had passed. They were slowly being turned into the drones they were always meant to be.

Mr Fox waited for his sister at the school gates and he watched every single child leave the school but his sister never appeared, so he decided to catch up with his friend Stanley. Both of them were too afraid to say anything, just in case somebody somewhere was watching them. Stanley turned down Livingstone road to go to his house and Mr Fox continued alone, he watched the streets slowly empty as everyone made their way into their bleak homes, until he found his own. Once inside he quietly looked around for his sister and carefully listened out for any noises that may have come from his parents bedroom, but there was nothing, there was not Arty Grape and there were no warm sounds filling the house. He knew something was wrong but he didn't want to admit it to himself, he knew his sister would not return and he fought back the tears when he realised he may never see her again.

It was starting to get dark outside and he was still waiting for his sister in the hallway, he sat there hoping he would hear the key in the door at any moment, his back ached as he slouched over himself on the floor. He had no idea what the time was, the clock in the hallway had been removed, only a dirty outline remained where it had once been, he could only guess how long he had been waiting for his sister, but he couldn't even use the sun to do that. His stomach began to ache and gurgle at the same time, he needed food and he couldn't wait for his sister any longer. Mr Fox crept into the kitchen to find some food, but to his dismay, when he opened one of the cupboards he found all the food had been removed, just like the clock. Somebody had removed every little bite and Mr Fox knew full well who the somebody was. He opened the other cupboards one by one, and one by one he discovered they had all been emptied apart from a single loaf of bread left in the cupboard by the side of the oven. They say that man cannot live on bread alone, but Mr Fox proved that theory wrong. He decided to make himself some toast, he popped two pieces of bread in and he stared into the reflective surface of the toaster whilst he waited for it to release his food; he saw himself, but he didn't recognised who he was in the distorted reflection of himself.

Oh, jeepers creepers, where'd ya get those peepers?
Jeepers creepers, where'd ya get those eyes?

The factory on the hill began to pump music into air again, it felt like it had always been there, the tune had become stuck in the mind of Mr Fox, he didn't know why it had suddenly started to play but he knew it was responsible for the bad things that were happening in the town of Eden. He sat there eating his dry toast, staring out of the window wondering what he was going to do, wondering when he would see his sister again, wondering if his parents would ever return to their normal selves. He listened to the music playing and he sang the words in his head. *Oh, jeepers creepers, where'd ya get those peepers? Jeepers creepers, where'd ya get those eyes?* A sudden panic swept over him, he realised that he had homework the needed to complete, so he rushed to find his bag, then he rushed to the table, and he frantically pulled out the homework he needed to finish. Mr Fox had more homework than usual, he kept pulling papers out of his bag like a magician pulling out a never ending handkerchief from his hat. He sat down and he scribbled and scrawled onto the homework pages, there was no stopping him and he couldn't stop until it was all done. The small hands on the imaginary clock in his head whizzed around. It was getting later and later and Mr Fox was no closer to finishing the work that he was expected of him. He was driven by the thought of what would happen to him if he didn't complete his work. After he placed the final full stop at the end of his last sentence he passed out on top of a stack of homework papers and he drifted into his own private world; it was a world he didn't want to wake up from when things were going good, but it was also a world he couldn't wake up from when things going bad. He created anxiety in what once were his peaceful dreams, he saw the vicious faces of his once kind teachers shouting at him, he was chased in slow motion down the corridors of his school only to be met with more monsters with every door he opened. Soon his nightmares would be over as the sun seeped through the window in the house piercing his eyelids and gradually waking him up. He slowly opened his eyes to a new day and the first thing he felt was a pencil digging into his cheek, burrowing itself slowly into his face like a tick. He had fallen asleep on all kinds of uncomfortable stationery that had left their mark. He pulled his carcass from the table, he was more disoriented than usual he usually was. *It must have been time for school* he thought but he only had the clock in his head as a reference. He gathered up his things and stuffed them into his bag before heading out the door for another day of the same things. The children flooded the streets once again, their eyes faced down, their shoulders hunched over, all were following each other and not knowing why. They had become unrecognisable, they had become a lost thought of their former selves. It was like the very blind leading the blind.

As the children walked silently to the only place they thought they should go, they prayed to a god that didn't exist and they asked him for help, but they found that god didn't want to help them anymore, god had left this world to the devil and the children were now beginning to realise.

Mr Fox found his way to school and when he reached the school gates he became hesitant to enter, but he had nowhere else to go. What would he do he thought, would he hide in his home with his strange parents lurking around for the rest of his life or would he carry on as normal like everyone else hoping that tomorrow would bring something new. He decided to pass through the gates and find his way to his classroom--again. Miss Cardownie Clare was waiting for him as he entered, she stood at the back of the room staring forward, he could only assume she was waiting for all the children to be seated before she began to torment them. She was such a beautiful teacher, she was his first and his favourite. Miss Cardownie Clare was older than most of the other teachers, but with age she brought her own kind of wisdom, she loved children, which is why she had taught them for such a long time. Unfortunately for Mr Fox even Miss Cardownie Clare could not fight the evil that lingered in the air, only the pure were spared. I He slowly made his way to his desk and he sat still and quiet like all the other children, waiting for Miss Cardownie Clare, who was waiting for every child to gave her the attention she required.

'Bring me your homework!' she screamed. Those words echoed down all the classrooms, all the corridor and by all the teachers in the schools across the town of Eden. The children stood and followed each other like sheep to lay down their homework upon Miss Cardownie Clare's desk. Any child that didn't hand in their homework suffered a fate worse than homework.

'Bring me your homework!'
'Bring me your homework!'
'Bring me your homework!'
'Bring me your homework!'
'Bring me your homework!'

Mr Fox stood in line, waiting to hand over his homework that he had stayed up all night to do, his mind was foggy and he thought he was living a dream, but despite how much he thought his situation was real, he knew that it was. As he stepped little by little towards the desk he thought about his sister. He had been distracted by everything else to give her a moments thought, but as soon as his mind cleared slightly he could see her face and he began wondering where she had gone and then it struck him, there was only one place she could have been taken and he felt stupid for not realising it sooner. She had been taken to the factory on the hill, where she would remain forever more. Once every piece of homework had been handed in and Miss Cardownie Clare was satisfied the children were given further instructions.

'Get up!'

'Walk out of the classroom!'

'Go to the great hall'

'Do not talk to anyone!'

'We are watching you!'

'GO NOW!' were the last words Miss Cardownie Clare shouted before the children left to their feet and hurried out of the room. As the children marched down the corridors they heard the screams of others, and they watched them being dragged off whilst doing nothing to stop the terrible things that they witnessed.

Everyone walked down the dark corridors, Mr Fox followed the person in front of him, who was following the person in front of them. He was suddenly blinded by the light as the doors at the end of the corridor were opened. As his eyes re-adjusted to the light, he found himself outside and there he could see child after child being carted into the back of the school minibuses. The seats had been removed from the back to make room for as many children as possible. Every teacher took part in the dirty deeds that were afoot; they performed their new duty without a moments hesitation. Soon this would become a normal thing to see, at first it shocked Mr Fox and the children, they couldn't believe the things they were witnessed with their own eyes, but eventually it became a normal sight to see.

The end of another day approached and Mr Fox still didn't have any answers. The things that were happening were still left unexplained, but he realised one thing; Mr Fox knew he had to find his sister.

Half Way There

Today is the day Mr Fox would be reunited with his sister, he would find her again, they would talk, they would laugh and they would cry together. They would give each other the biggest hug that they had ever given each other, they would tell each other how much they loved each other before it was too late. Unfortunately today wasn't that day and Arty Grape and Mr Fox would soon forget each other even existed if they didn't remind themselves.

The children found themselves back in their classrooms again, sitting on the same seats they had sat on each day. The teachers shouted the same words they had shouted at them yesterday and the day before that.

'Bring me your homework!'

'Bring me your homework!'

'Bring me your homework!'

'Bring me your homework!'

'Bring me your homework!'

One by one the children brought their homework, they dragged their feet as they walked to the desk at the front of every classroom, they were tired, they were fed up but their lifeless bodies were somehow able to carry on. Mr Fox stood up and joined the orderly queue yet again, it was his turn to hand in his homework, but when that time came he just stood there defiant, not knowing what he was doing, but really he did. Miss Morrison stared at him, waiting for him to lay the pages upon the desk. She waited and she waited before standing up and towering over him. 'Bring me your homework!' she shouted, but Mr Fox did no such thing and before he know it he was dragged away. His feet skidded across the wooden floor as he was pulled by the back of his jumper and forced against his will down the corridor and through the heavy doors that separated him from the outside world. The sun struck his eyes and burned his retinas, he was blinded momentarily and when he could see, he wished that he couldn't because he could see the fate that awaited him. The school minibus was waiting for him and he became just like all the other children that were being loaded into the back of it. There was no escape and even if he did escape he didn't know where to go. He was thrown aboard and surrounded by other children until other children were thrown aboard and surounded him, slowly he didn't have any room to move let alone breathe. Child after child was thrown towards him until there was no more room left. The doors of the minibus were slammed shut and its engine stirred. It was time for them to be taken away; the town of Eden would soon become a distant memory to them, they would soon have different troubles to overcome.

The minibus drove slowly down many of the main roads in the town of Eden, he gazed through the armpits of the many children crammed onto the minibus watching the trees and the town pass by. Finally it turned off into an unnamed side road that Mr Fox would often cycle down, which led to the start of the glorious mountains. He had become convinced that he saw the NoWhereMan standing on the side of the road as the bus quickly passed but. The NoWhereMan watched as the minibus drove past and he chose not to intervene. *Why didn't the NoWhereMan help?* thought Mr Fox.

Mr Fox felt the minibus being to slow, it stopped at the entrance to the mountain climb, the invisible gatekeepers had yet to give their answers. The driver pulled up the handbrake and he turned off the engine and he waited for whatever answers were about to come. The silence felt like forever, and then it broken by the driver violently slamming his hands on the horn three times. The horn screamed and the children screamed in surprise too. On his third strike he held the horn down and he growled like a wild animal, which frightened the children even more. He sat up like nothing had happened and he released the handbrake before turning the engine and continuing to drive into the mountain where the trees and the darkness soon engulfed them all.

The minibus weaved around the winding roads of the mountain, it carefully navigated every treacherous corner and stayed away from all the danger the mountain brought. Animals were wandering the unmarked road, mountain streams flowed and deep ditches tempted the minibus towards a horrible fate. It was cold and dark inside the minibus and the children were scared, some were sobbing silently to themselves, others had a deathly stare of fear in their eyes; fear was the only thing that kept them company on their trip to the factory on the hill. They drifted round and round the mountain path as the they climbed higher and higher to their eventual doom. The forest didn't let any light through its impenetrable foliage, it had decided to deny the children of any favour. The children soon became used to the darkness that had begun to form inside and around them. The darkness filled the minibus and then the trees disappeared from above them and the light momentarily poured into the minibus again, they were momentarily surrounded by the hopeful light and then it was gone. They were getting closer to the factory on the hill.

The minibus kept winding around the roads and it finally

reached the top of the mountain. In the distance stood the tall gates of the factory that was reluctant to let anybody in or out. The gates became taller and taller the closer they travelled and then they slowly began to open, it was as if they had anticipated the approach of the minibus, the children were finally welcomed to a place they didn't want to be. Everything came to a halt, even Mr Fox's heart stopped and time seemed to stand still. Everyone waited in the silence that filled the air, they had reached their final destination.

Mr Fox struggled to look through the window to see a building illuminated by its own light. He saw a man standing in front of it with his arms folded behind his back, and this man watched the minibus with great intent. He stood in front of an open door and the light behind him cast him into a silhouette, he was the shadow that he wanted to be. The silhouetted man raised his arm to signal the driver and the driver immediately jumped out of his seat and ran to the back of the minibus flinging its doors open. He dragged the children off the minibus as quickly as they had been put on, and he lined them up in the courtyard of the factory on the hill. As soon as Mr Fox was dragged from the minibus he started to look for the silhouetted man, but he had gone, all that was left was the light emanating from the doorway. Mr Fox knew that the silhouetted man was behind the strange things that were occurring and he was going to find out why, but first he had to find his sister. His thoughts were quickly interrupted but two people that burst through the door of the factory on the hill, as they approached him he realised that he recognised one of them. It was Stanley's mum, but from the look in her eyes he knew that she wasn't Stanley's mum anymore. The children were quickly blindfolded, and every child was made to hold the shoulder of the person in front of them, before they played their last deadly game of follow the leader. The only thing Mr Fox could see was the darkness that stared back at him, the only sounds he could hear were the different vibrations of his footsteps walking across the different types of floors he encountered. He kept following his leader, he went upstairs, then downstairs, he was turned around and tied into knots, and then a hand grabbed him hard and pushed him in another direction. He was pushed forwards, sideways, left and right until he was eventually brought to a stop. Mr Fox wasn't holding the shoulders of another child anymore, he had found himself all alone. The hand that held him grabbed him hard and it commanded him not to move. He was spun around and he was left standing there with his blindfold firmly in its place. Nothing was said and he didn't dare move, he had no idea where he had been taken to--Do You? Let's make this up as we go shall we and see where it ends. I might need your help along the way, but we will get to the end eventually.

Chapter Fourteen

It was night time and Arty Grape had no other choice but to sleep, she would be asleep for many more hours unbeknown to her. She lay there very still in her uncomfortable bed, nothing but her dreams mattered. She smiled gently to herself through the many hours of her dreams, at random intervals she would talk out loud to herself, asking and answering her own questions. The sun started to creep up from behind horizon and the light began to change, but Arty Grape didn't know that was happening. She carefully stirred herself awake. *I wonder if I have awoken from my nightmare?* she thought. *I know I'm awake but how do I know I am awake, I thought I was awake in my dream, but now I know I am awake* she thought again. *This isn't a dream, this is really happening.* When Arty Grape woke she found herself in a room that she had been placed in the night before. She had been blindfolded and led there by a commanding hand. She didn't know who had put her there and she didn't remember falling asleep, the last thing she remembered was being blind folded and left to her own devices, occupying a space and a time.

She sat up on the edge of a bed, the metal frame dug into her skin leaving an imprint that she would always remember. She pulled her blindfold down and looked around the room, she realised she couldn't see a door, she was trapped, there was no way out and she didn't know how she had found her way in. A crackled voice spoke through one of the speakers fitted in the corner of the room. 'It's time.' said the voice.

Arty Grape kept staring at the speaker on the wall, she couldn't tear her eyes away, she began to look around the empty room that she found herself in. Concrete wall surrounded her and nothing else, it was like a prison cell that she had been allocated, but a prison cell without a door. She kept glancing around the room trying to figure out how she had got into it and it was only after looking around for the seventh time did she see a door. *Had it always been there* she thought whilst she stared through it. Arty Grape continued to stare through the door that had only just appeared until she realised she had no other choice but to step through it and see what delights greeted her on the other side. She carefully stepped towards the exit of the room and peered for the first time into the factory on the hill. It was vast and she became overwhelmed by its size. Directly across from her she could see other children doing the same thing, some looked scared and some looked like they were used to the situation they found themselves in. There were multiple floors above and below Arty Grape, all stretching as far as the eye could see, and all filled with the pitiful children of the town of Eden. Arty Grape wished for her own bed, her own room, to see her brother again and to be hugged by her mama and papa. She wanted to believe that she was living in a dream, a dream of her own making, but it wasn't, it wasn't a dream and she wouldn't wake up for a very long time.

'Prepare.' commanded the voice. Arty Grape watched all the children swiftly turn to the right. 'Continue.' It spoke again. Every child began to walk along the metal gantry and Arty Grape didn't know what to do as she stood dazed and confused. She had no choice but to follow the others as they marched to their unknown destination. They marched and they marched like ten thousand men through the factory. Along the way they were fed their breakfast, it was a badly toasted bun with wet scrambled egg dripping out of the sides, the filthy juice dripped down Arty Grape's hand and it made her stomach want to heave. All the children had to eat what they were given and Arty Grape soon found out that it was always wet scrambled egg in a badly toasted bun, every single day. Dotted around the factory Arty Grape could see the parents of many of the children, they kept their watchful eyes on them at all times. Hundreds upon hundreds of children followed each other, it was like a factory filled with animals waiting to be slaughtered and not knowing what was coming next. They led one another down the tight staircases and they worked their way to the main room where a sea of desks and chairs waited for them to sit and obey the orders that were given to them from up on high.

Each child found a place to sit and as Arty Grape followed them they would sit down and disappear and then she would follow the next child that was in front of her. She began to panic, she began to think about finding her place, where would she sit, was there a place for her and if there wasn't, what would she do. On every level of the factory Arty Grape could see the parents of all the children, there stood Issy's dad and over there stood Jocobs mum. They were staring over everyone, watching them intently, waiting for someone to make a mistake so that they could take them away to the next horrible place. Every child seemed to be closely monitored by the adults that surrounded them, their strange eyes were upon them at all times, burrowing slowly into their self esteem, eating what little of them that was left.

The children found their seats and they sat nicely waiting for their next instruction. Without hesitation they opened their drawers and picked up their pens and pencisand they worked their way through the stack of white pages that waited for them, just like every other day. Some of the children had been there longer than others and everything seemed like a normal thing to do, but Arty Grape was still waiting to wake up. One by one they scribbled on the white pages as she walked past, still trying to find her seat and her place in this new world. Arty Grape didn't know what to do with herself once she found a spare chair, so she did exactly the same as all the other children. She picked up one of the white pages and began to answer the questions it asked.

'Its okay Arty Grape. Its okay.' spoke the voice from the white page. 'Everything will be fine, you'll see, everything will be as fine as you want it to be, it will be just like that day you promised you would never forget.' Arty Grape continued to stare at the white pages for a little longer. She stared and she stared until a hand grabbed her hard from behind, immediately she was pulled out of her day dream and back into reality. She turned to look at the owner of the hand that grabbed her. When she looked up and her eyes adjusted she realised it was her father, she was so happy to see him until she realised he wasn't happy to see her. Arty Grape looked at him and he looked back at her with a hateful look in his eyes that she had never seen before. He violently grabbed a pile of the white pages in his hand and he slammed them down on the desk, and then he pushed Arty Grape hard into the desk, her ribs hit the table edge, sending a shooting pain directly into the pain receptors of her brain. He stood over her, intimidating her with his presence whilst pointing at the white pages that lay upon her desk. Arty Grape had no other choice, she reached for the page at the top of the pile and placed it neatly on the desk besides the pile. Her father pointed at the draw in the desk and Arty Grape immediately opened it, fearing what he would do if she didn't. Inside she found pens and pencils and she grabbed a black pen directly in front of her and began to look at the white pages. This seemed to satisfy her father, who then moved down the aisle and began watching over all the other children, making sure they were being obedient the the will of the factory on the hill. *Nobody is coming for me* thought Arty Grape. *I'll never leave this place.* She sat for hours working her way through the white pages, her arm ached, her fingers began to blister from holding the pen for hours upon hours.

'103485372' crackled a voice from the large speakers hanging from the factory walls.

Arty Grape didn't know what the numbers meant, and she wouldn't find out until she graced the pages of another story.

Unbeknown to her, she was being assimilated into all the other children, resistance was futile. Every child in the room would soon stop thinking for themselves, every child in the room was becoming like each other. A broken, worn down version of what they once were. The white pages flowed with great abundance, warping their minds with every page they turned, staring back at them and shaping their every thought.

The children hadn't been in the factory long, yet their personalities had been taken from them before they even had a chance to find them, snatched in the night by a clever thief, but Arty Grape was determined not to let the same thing happen to her. Arty Grape's papa had always repeated to her: *focus, determination, concentration* and whilst she was a guest of the factory on the hill, she remembered those three things. Every day she would pretend to look like she was obeying every command that was given to her but she was just waiting for the moment she could change things.

The days passed and the routine had started to become just that. Arty Grape had become an actress in her own play, playing the part of a prisoner trapped in her own existence.

'98187745362' spoke the voice.

Arty Grape tried hard to keep track of the days that had drifted past her but it was getting increasingly harder. *Today is Tuesday* she thought out loud as she worked her way through the white pages. Arty Grape had figured out that there was always a delivery of fresh children on Tuesday, or at least she had convinced herself it always happened on Tuesday, in reality she didn't know what day it was or how long she had been there.

The arrival of the new children had become the only thing that broke up the monotony of existing in the factory on the hill. Arty Grape had noticed that the children became more alert when they arrived, like Pavlov's dog waiting for a treat, they became excited when the heard the locks on the large doors at the front of the factory turn. The sound echoed through the large room and the children began to salivate. They would sit up and stretch their bodies, their spines clicked into a position long forgotten. The large doors in the hall swung open and in came the next batch of slaves. They were blindfolded just like Arty Grape had been when she had arrived, one by one the frightened children were taken to their empty rooms, and one by one they would wake up in the morning without remembering how they fell asleep. As they were marched to their new homes she would always look up very carefully. Arty Grape would see the young ones sobbing and the older ones fighting back their tears. She didn't recognise any of them because she couldn't see their eyes. She kept glancing at each and every one of them as they walked through the factory, her eyes darted from left to right and then from right to left again and again. Her eyes were seeing things quicker than her brain could process and she often thought her eyes were playing tricks on her, she often thought she saw her brother being marched through the factory on the hill, and then she realised a cruel trick had been played on her, but not today. Out of the corner of her eyes she saw him, she recognised his hair, nobody had hair like her brother in the town of Eden, it was large and wild, just like he had wanted it to be. She followed him with her eyes as much as she could without drawing attention to herself, but eventually lost track of him as he moved up and down the many staircases in the factory, he became lost amongst the sea of desperate children.

Arty Grape had glanced upon the sweet face of her brother once again, his beautiful face had filled her with a new hope.

'1056784738' spoke the voice.

Chapter Fifteen

Mr Fox woke up in a room; he was confused and disoriented. He removed the thin blanket that been placed upon him and he sat on the edge of a metal framed bed. He looked around the room that he found himself in and he noticed the absence of everything, even a door. He sat and he wondered how he had got there and how he had entered a room that had no door. He could remember everything from the night before; the minibus, the mountain, the silhouetted man, he could remember everything apart from getting into bed and falling asleep. He could even remember why he had wanted to be taken to the factory on the hill, he remembered that he needed to find his sister.

'It's time.' spoke the voice.

Mr Fox jumped up from the bed at the sound of the voice, he was startled and he wondered where it had come from. He looked around the room but saw nothing and then he looked at the place he had always been looking, to his surprise he saw an opening in the wall that wasn't there before. Through the opening he could see children standing on walkways in the vast factory on the hill. He cautiously made his way outside of the room and looked around. He could see hundreds of children standing outside their rooms, they stood straight and they stood still, like they were waiting for their next command. Mr Fox was in awe of the size of the factory on the hill, above him were hundreds of children and below him there were even more.

'Prepare.' spoke the voice.

The children immediately turned as they heard the voice, and they began to walk along the walkways of the factory. Like little ants they followed each other, Mr Fox assumed they all knew where they were going, so he followed them too. He walked along the metal floors that floated high above the factory, along the way he found himself holding a bread roll with scrambled egg in his hand, it had been thrust into his hand without him knowing, he hated scrambled egg, he was disgusted by the sight--What Mr Fox didn't realised was that he would soon be eating scrambled egg every day and he would be grateful for every little bite he could get.

His eyes darted around the huge building, he hoped that he would spot his sister amongst the other lost souls, but he couldn't, there were too many children for him to count. He realised that he hadn't thought his plan through very well and now he had become trapped in the walls of the factory like everybody. He came to the factory to save his sister but now he needed saving too.

Just like Arty Grape he soon found himself sitting at a desk staring at the white pages. He still had his bread roll in his hand, dripping with scrambled egg juice that had left a trail on the floor and across his hands. He didn't know what to do so he copied what the other children did. He opened the draw in the desk and he pulled out a pen like all the other children did, but before he had a chance to close the drawer, it was slammed shut by somebody else. He was grabbed hard from behind and his bread roll was snatched from him and forced into his mouth. A woman stood over him and stared deep into his eyes, he needed to eat his disgusting food and he needed to do it as quickly as he could. He gasped for air with every foul bite until he swallowed the last hideous soggy piece. Once he had swallowed the last bite, he was instructed to pick up the pen he had placed on the desk and begin the work that would never end. The same routine befell Mr Fox as it had his sister. He would work his way through the white pages for the rest of his time, he was now under the spell of the factory on the hill but just like Arty Grape he would pretend for as long as it took him to find his sister. Mr Fox had a plan, but he was only foolish enough to think about the first part of it, not its second, he didn't know what was coming next. He knew he needed to find his sister but he also needed to stay alive. God had begun to laugh at the plan he had and Mr Fox didn't even believe in God. As the days passed, finding his sister began to feel like an impossible task and he began to wonder if she was even in the factory on the hill. *There was nowhere else she could have been taken* he thought *but I can't be sure of that.*

Every day he sat at a desk and he worked his way through the white pages until it was time to be marched back to a room again, he would always try to mark the walls somehow, he hoped one day to discover his own words written on the walls.

As each day left him it became harder and harder for him to carry on. His demeanour was being slowly dragged to the ground, he hadn't seen daylight for a very long time and it began to effect his mood, he lived in solitary most of the time, even when he was around other people. A sadness began to fall over Mr Fox and it took time for him to shake it off. Whilst his heart felt heavy, he contemplated all the things he would do if he were to leave the factory on the hill. He thought about the clean air he would breathe, he thought about the laughter he would hear in the streets and he thought about the blue sky and the clouds. Day after day passed him by and he still hadn't seen his sister.

Mr Fox found himself at the edge of his bed once again, he had sat there so many times and stared at the walls that madness had begun to settle in and take hold. He stood up and he walked to the corner of the room and he began to speak to it.

'Hi. How are you? What are you doing here? I'm not sure what happened to me, I just woke up one day and I found myself here. How about you? Strange isn't it? Strange that one minute you wake up and you are there and then one day you wake up you are here. I don't know what's happening, do you?' Mr Fox knew he wouldn't receive a response from the wall but he kept talking to it as much as he could, it had become his only friend. His insanity started to creep up on him even further.

'My name is Fox and I am trying to find my sister Arty Grape. I know you can hear me. My name is Mr Fox and I am trying to find my sister Arty Grape. Have you seen her, do you know her, do you know where she is?' Mr Fox pleaded with the wall every night but it was hopeless, the wall would never answer him. He soon realised he was on his own in the factory on the hill and he would be on his own until he escaped its walls. He laid down on his bed and he let his mind wander to other things again. He thought about his sisters' smile, he thought about his mamas laugh and he thought about all the joyful memories that would help place a smile on his sullen face. Slowly his brain began to switch off, he was so tired that he dreamt he was asleep, Mr Fox dreamt that he was dreaming.

'It's time.' crackled the voice.

It was morning again and Mr Fox was still deep in his sleep, he would normally wake before the voice spoke, but not today, the voice would bring him back into the world. His eyes flickered open and he laid still on his bed staring up at the ceiling. The invisible door was already open and he found himself running to it, readying himself for the day he had been programmed to fulfil. He jumped out of bed and sped out to the walkway, standing there with all the other children, waiting for his next instruction. He lifted his shoulders, then his chin and gazed directly ahead, his eyes never wavered from a spot he would always look at across the large expanse. Something felt different today, it took him several moments to realise what it was. When he focused his eyes he could see his sister as clear as the day, she was standing right in front of him and she was a sight for his sore eyes. Arty Grape was staring right back at him, she had been waiting for him to notice her. They both found each others' gaze and everything suddenly felt okay. All the hardship they had suffered had been wiped away with a single smile. A tear escaped from Mr Fox's eye, he hadn't felt any emotion for a long time and it reminded him that he was human, he realised that if one tear could escape then a thousand more would follow. They kept smiling at each other, they now knew they weren't on their own anymore.

'Prepare.' said the voice and then the children turned and marched. Mr Fox lost sight of his sister again as the children followed their daily orders.

The children found a different desk every different day, and they worked their way through the white pages that rested on their table of things. The day ended as quickly as it had begun but the day felt different for Mr Fox and Arty Grape. They had another reason to keep going or to keep carrying on. They knew they had each other, and they held on to the thought that one day they would be reunited again. But the days kept passing and the reasons to find each other kept slipping away. Mr Fox had lost count of the number of times he had marched to a desk, he had forgotten how many times he had looked around himself. Eventually he would stop looking for his sister, he would just sit and he would work his way through the endless white pages that kept coming, taunting him with every page that he turned. His eyes had glazed over a long time ago and his mind had begun to ask how long it could carry on? When Mr Fox finally told himself he couldn't go on anymore; he heard his namel gently uttered by his side.

'Fox.' the voice whispered. 'Fox!' it whispered again. He carefully glanced to his side without moving his head, his eyeballs began to hurt as they reached the point that they couldn't go any further. 'Fox!' the voice said one more time, and this time he recognised the sweet tones of his sisters voice. He turned his head very slowly and slightly to his side to see if it really was his sister calling his name. Out of the corner of his eye he recognised the burry shape of his sister, he had found Arty Grape.

'Don't look at me.' she gently whispered.

'I never thought I'd see you again.' said Arty Grape.

'Me too.' said Mr Fox.

'Are you okay Fox?'

'I'm okay. Are you okay Arty?'

'I'm okay.'

'How are we going to get out of here? How will I find you again? What's happening? questioned Mr Fox.

'I don't know. We'll figure it out.'

Chapter Sixteen

It was the third day in the factory on the hill and Arty Grape had been accustomed to the routine, she had been accustomed to certain things that had started to happen. Arty Grape had been watching everything very closely, she soon realised that on the third day a cloaked man began to appear. This man would stand high above the children, his face would always be obscured by the distance he had created between them. Nobody knew what he looked like, but Arty Grape was determined to discover who the maker of her current world was. The cloaked man paced backwards and forwards across the walkway on the top floor of the factory, occasionally stopping to look down on everyone. It felt like he was making sure everything was going according to his plan, not a page out of line or a single child astray. It looked like he was carefully counting his children, like a miser would count his golden coins. Day by day the factory filled with unsuspecting children, each child having their childhood snatched from them as they passed through the factory doors.

Arty Grape had been watching the cloaked man as much as she possible could, she had started to see a routine in everything that was happening. Like clockwork the cloaked man walked across the gantry, and like clockwork he stopped to count the children before disappearing down a corridor and never to be seen again. Until the next third day.

Arty Grape started to notice other things too that the other children hadn't even thought about, she noticed that the guards in in the factory had started to diminish, the number of people monitoring the children had decreased, their numbers were becoming less and less. It had happened so slowly that it had become unnoticed by her for some time. The children in the factory didn't need watching anymore, they were no longer thinking for themselves, they had been sufficiently controlled with the threat of an imagined fear, that's all it took to keep them in line. The children w ho had disappeared from the town of Eden had been brought to the factory on the hill--*but where did they go after they were taken from the factory,* Arty Grape asked herself.

The children had succumbed to the white pages and their daily routine, they had no choice but to keep going. They never spoke to each other and they dared not make eye contact, they all knew that they didn't exist anymore, to each other or to themselves. They were mere commodities in a very twisted marketplace.

Arty Grape worked her way through the white pages, letting her thoughts wonder as they flowed. She thought about how she could escape the factory on the hill and find her brother. Whilst she plundered her thoughts for happy memories, a plan of escape walked into the headquarters of her ideas. Arty Grape was slightly annoyed that it had taken her so long to think of it and she soon realised it was because she wasn't brave enough to do it. Like all the other children she encountered, Arty Grape was also too scared to talk whilst living in the factory on the hill, but she realised she didn't need to talk, all she needed to do was to do was use the written word and place it upon the white pages she had been forced to look at every single day.

Arty Grape would begin writing messages inside every white page that was presented to her on each day. She would write little notes in the margins of the pages, hoping one day somebody would notice her silent screams.

Is this you Fox? – Arty

--Arty would look back on that sentence. She would look back and always remember the first thing she wrote.

The first thing Arty Grape thought to do was to reach out to find her brother, she wanted to let him know that she wcas thinking of him.

Is there anybody out there? Can you hear me? she scribbled again.

Arty Grape kept writing messages on the white pages every day, it became her only purpose, finally her life had meaning, but it still made no sense. Every day Arty Grape wrote messages of all the things she wanted to say and to ask, she wanted to leave the factory on the hill but she couldn't do it alone. Arty Grape needed all the other children to join her fight. Day after day she wrote messages, and day after day it felt like she was writing in vain. Days passed and one thousand words had been written and one thousand words would never return. Arty Grape grew in frustration, she didn't know how long she could go on fighting the negative forces that surrounded her. Slowly the negativity would work its way into the empty spaces in her mind, gnawing away at any brain matter that wasn't strong enough to resist. Arty Grape became exhausted by the waiting, she began having thoughts about giving up, she just wanted to crawl under a rock and go to sleep for an eternity+*1*.

Arty Grape was, slowly yet surely, becoming just like all the other children, she couldn't fight it anymore, she didn't want to fight it, she was desperate to give in to its will. She had given up all hope of ever leaving, or of things ever going back to normal again. Arty Grape had become a prisoner of her own relentless thoughts--Where had all the beautiful children gone, the little souls who had laughed and smiled all day and every day, the people that played without a care in the world.

Arty Grape woke up in her cell, she laid still on top of the thin and uncomfortable mattress, staring at the ceiling. She didn't move her eyes, for there was nothing to see anymore. The isolation was bearing down on her shoulders like an unreasonable man, waiting for her to yield. Arty Grape had a small grasp on what was left of her existence, she was slowly moving to the edge of her thoughts where she would be taken to another place that she didn't want to go.

'It's time.' spoke the voice.

Arty Grape groaned inside as she rolled out of her bed and stepped out of her room, like she usually did.

'Prepare.' spoke the voice.

She followed the rest of the children as they moved through, and down the factory, and then she found her way to a desk and ploughed her way through the next pile of white pages, slowly working through her dark thoughts at the same time. She sat for hours turning page after page. She had stopped looking for messages, even her own, until a message came.

Is this you Arty Grape?

Chapter Seventeen

Mr Fox hadn't seen his beautiful sister since the very day that he found himself next to her. He missed her infectious laugh, he missed her weirdness which she wore on her sleeve like a badge of honour. He longed to see her smile again, he too lived in hope of being reunited, but with every sun that set brought him more disappointment. Mr Fox decided he couldn't sit and do nothing anymore, he had to do something, else he would be a fool, and not even a fool does nothing he thought. Like his sister and all the other children, he was marched back into his room at the end of each day. He would crawl his way into his bed and lay there looking up at the ceiling. He stared out loud and he dreamed the morning away, unknowingly waiting for the morning to arrive. As soon as he woke he felt an energy that he hadn't felt for a long time. Mr Fox felt a purpose rising up through his body that he hadn't felt for a long time. He marched down to a desk with all the other children, but today he had a purpose in his heart. The white pages taunted him from the desk., just like they had taunted him every other day, but everything felt different to him today. *Why haven't I thought about this before?* he wondered amongst himself. It was a perfectly simple and such an easy thing to do, but I didn't do it and I didn't even think it he thought to himself again. Mr Fox decided to leave his very own message, in the white pages, to his sister or to anyone that didn't want to avert their innocent eyes. He hoped that he would be heard, and he hoped that just one other person would be inspired to leave their own message, reassuring the next person that they were not alone.

Mr Fox grabbed a white page from the stack and he scrawled a message carefully, quietly and secretly. He left message after message to his sister and to anyone that was listening.

> *Is this you Arty?- Fox*
> *I'm still here Arty. I'm looking for you - Fox.*
> *Look for me - Fox*
> *This has to stop - Fox*
> *We have to do something - Fox*

His messages started to turn to madness, like a prayer to an imaginary God. Days had passed since he had written his first message to his beautiful sister but he didn't receive a single response. The energy that he started to feel began to slip away. The third day would come and go

Slowly his new found energy and purpose began to slip away. The third day had come and gone several times, and each time the cloaked man looked down his nose upon them once again. He never hid his disgust that he had for the children, even though he was once one of them, it was a hatred that couldn't be contained, it was a hatred that gave birth to his original evil plan to hurt others as much as he could.

Mr Fox worked his way through the dense white pages, they would haunt him when he was awake and they haunted him in his dreams, there was no escaping all the questions he had to answer. He pulled another page from the white pile and there in front of him lay a message that he thought he had never written. It took him several moments before he could decipher his own handwriting and determine what the message said.

'127863723' spoke the voice.

Mr Fox looked up and to the front of the factory, a large clock was suspended in the expanse of the factory, it was there for everyone to see, it told the time, it told the hour and the minute but it never told the day. A small hand worked its way around the face of the clock, as he watched it he realised for the first time that the numbers flowed in a different direction than he had expected.

He didn't feel like writing any more messages on the white pages. *What was the point?* he thought, and at that moment, you know that moment, like in the movies when everything seems lost but the person is saved--that moment.

Mr Fox discovered a message hiding at the bottom of one of the white pages, where he never usually looked. He didn't know who the message was from because there person had forgotten to leave their name. It could have been his sister, or it could have been one of the multitudes of lost children wandering around the factory. He carefully looked around with his eyes and listened to any ominous footsteps that might be coming his way, before he scribbled a message back on to the white pages.

Is this you Arty? We need to leave this place, we need to escape!

He wrote and he wrote different messages every moment he had, and it wasn't long before the messages started flooding back to him, it was as if a tap had been turned on and it couldn't be turned off. Letters, words and sentences flooded the factory floor through every desolate word of the white page.

Who are you?
Where are we?
Why are we?
What should we do?

How do we escape?
Is anybody listening?

The sounds of all the words echoed from the white pages and through the factory. The children could feel the unrest coming, they could hear it as the wavelength of their feelings bounced off ever wall.

Every child carried on marching back and forth and from place to place, keeping quiet as they moved, they didn't want to arouse any suspicion--it was a secret after all, that the end was coming--Children are clever you see, adults think that they are much smarter than children, but they're not! Adults are clever in different ways and children are clever in all the other wonderful ways.

More of the slow days passed, and as they did, more and more of the children began to feel stronger. Hope had lifted their spirits, it had renewed their souls and given them a new vigour that they would carry forth. They didn't feel alone anymore.

The messages had slowly worked their way around the factory without discovery, the cloaked man thought he had broken them but really he had underestimated them. Soon the messages found their way to where Arty Grape was sitting, she was sitting at a desk, she was dejected, she didn't know what more she could do until she turned to the first white page. She didn't notice the message at first, and when she did, Ary Grape had to control the smile on her face, she had to stop it from breaking out.

Is this you Arty? – Fox. spoke the message.

It was a message from her brother, she had hoped that her messages would find but she knew the probability of it happening was immeasurable. As she sat there controlling her smile, she realised it was impossible and immediately a beaming smile took over her face, her teeth shone and her cheek bones burst out of their caverns. Arty Grape had to throw her hand over her mouth otherwise she would be discovered, no child smiled in the factory on the hill, if they did, they would be deemed insane, and immediately taken away. Arty Grape wanted to cry but she didn't know if the tears would be of sadness or of joy, she had to control herself once again or face detection.

I'm here Fox and I'm coming to find you she wrote. *Wait for the third day.*

Over and over Arty Grape began to write messages. Every day, every second and every heart beat she had, was spent thinking about the messages she could write, she didn't care who was listening all she cared about was writing--and that's when the madness began to set in.

There are more of us than there are of them.

We can overcome them.

Wait for the third day.

The cloaked man shall not control us.

There is no escape.

I am doomed.

The same messages kept coming back to her, but each without a name.

We can overcome them.

Wait for the third day.

The cloaked man shall not control us.

There is no escape.

Chapter Eighteen

Arty Grape was ready to discover the truth. If you lived in the factory with her and you observed her every move, you would see that she had changed. Her face had begun to glow again, she stood tall amongst the other children and her thoughts and her feelings that were once lost began to return to her. Arty Grape had also noticed that many more of the children that were once slouched over themselves, stood tall and proud, with a renewed look in their eyes. Hundreds and hundreds of children patiently waited for the dawn of the third day, they had seen it come and leave them so many times, but they knew it was coming, they just had to carry on until the time came.

Another morning arrived, Arty Grape woke up once again in her dirty cell where the isolation wrapped around her like a cold blanket. She muttered to herself like she usually did each morning, even though hope had returned to her heart, loneliness still crept in. She sat on the edge of her (cosy) bed, she remembered who she was, she remembered where she was and she remembered what she had to do. Every morning she always tried to remember who she lest she forget.

Arty Grape remembered that today was the day she would execute the first part of her *stupid and ridiculous plan*. She had thought about all the horrible consequences and she was still determined to follow it through--Isn't that nice.

'I'll have a glass of consequences please.'

'Are you sure?'

'Yes, I'm sure and please stop trying to tell me what to do!'

Arty Grape's little plan would seem foolish to the likes of me and you, but she was a clever little thing who didn't rush in like other fools.

'Time' spoke the speakers, and the door to her room materialised before her very eyes, it had done that a thousand times before and every time it happened always felt majestic to her. Arty Grape stood up and walked towards towards the door and stepped out on to the walkway. She marched to a desk like she usually did and with every little step that she took she felt things changing around her, she felt calm and she felt happy. It felt like she was in the last days of the factory--Then her happiness turned to negativity, it was like a swarm of bees had attacked her positive thoughts. *What if I fail?* she thought, and then an exponential amount of other dark thoughts flooded the frontal part of her hippopotamus. Arty Grape had to battle her through her thoughts, like a knight fighting the kings enemies. It was time for Arty Grape to execute her plan.

Arty Grape followed all the other sheep like children, but today was going to be different, she would only follow the children for a short amount of time. She cautiously followed them as they each tried to find a desk. Arty Grape was waiting for her moment to come, because when it did, she had mere seconds to execute the first part of her *ridiculous and stupid* plan. Every day that had passed until this moment, Arty Grape had been observing, she had been observing the factory, she had been observing the children and she had been observing the grown ups around the factory that had been watching her. She had liked to call them, in her own mind, the '???????'

The moment she had been waiting for was fast approaching and suddenly it arrived, she didn't have the option of hesitating, it was now or never for, she had no time to talk herself out if it, she had no time to think about whether or not what she was doing was a good idea. Arty Grape quickly slipped to the side and into a tiny black corridor she hadn't noticed was there for a very long time, but when she did, Arty Grape knew it had to be explored. She had left the walkway for the first time, she had stopped following the rest of her world. Arty Grape stood in the side corridor composing herself, watching the children march past. She turned her head to look the other way, down the corridor she found herself in, and there lay a dark spiral staircase ahead of her. She kept standing and breathing hard, eventually composing herself, preparing herself for the next part of her plan. Her senses became heightened by the sound of the children's feet marching, her heart pounded musical beats in her chest, she could feel the blood being pumped around her body and the adrenaline rushing through her veins. Arty Grape began to walk towards the spiral staircase, her legs carried her without consent. She could see the blank paint on the stairs peeling off and the rust slowly making it's way to every surface of the staircase. As she drew closer the palms of her hands began to sweat and she couldn't stop rubbing them on what had become to feel like a prison uniform.

Arty Grape looked down to examine her sweaty hands, but instead of water glistening off her palms, she was faced with the deepest and darkest colour of red; her hands were covered in blood, she had cut herself without even knowing. The blood kept dripping from her hand, there was nothing she could do, even thought it was a small cut, it didn't want to stop bleeding. As she walked down the corridor she realised she was leaving more blood than breadcrumbs. The corridor began to narrow as she got closer to the spiral staircase, each of her shoulders touched the wall on either side, the spiral staircase was directly in front of her, if she reached out she would be able to touch it. The steps shone in any light that it could attract from the dark factory. Arty Grape had past her point of no return, she looked up the spiral staircase and then she looked down, the stairs twisted a long way in both directions through the factory, Arty Grape already knew which way she was going to go, she was going up into the heavens of the factory, she was going to the seventh floor where the cloaked man resides. Arty Grape was going to find all the answers to her unanswered, questions.

She placed one foot on to the first step of the staircase, and step by step she began to ascend the mountain of stairs ahead of her, she needed to move fast, Arty Grape knew she only had a certain amount of time to implement the next part of her suicide mission. It was the third day and the cloaked man would be appearing shortly, Arty Grape needed to be ready for when he showed his shadowy face. She kept climbing the stairs until she reached the seventh floor, or at least what she had calculated to be the seventh floor, where the cloaked man would honour the children with his presence.

Down in the deep and dark depths of the factory floor the children found their way to a desk. Arty Grape was waiting for complete silence and then she waited for the sound of one hundred and too many white pages being turned over by the enslaved children. On the third day she had observed that the cloaked man would always appear shortly after the white pages being turned. Arty Grape was about to find out where the cloaked man had come from, so she eagerly awaited his appearance, only then could she execute her next cunning move.

Arty Grape walked away from the spiral staircase, it would become a distant memory to her--for now. She walked to the end of the corridor and crouched down, peering out as carefully as she could. Arty Grape had planned things perfectly, and as she had expected the cloaked man made his appearance exactly when she thought he would. She stood closer to him than she had ever imagined she would, and discovered he was taller than he looked. The cloaked man paced back and forth, stopping in the middle of the long walkway, like he usually did when he paid the children a visit. He would stop to glare upon the dirty children beneath him; Arty Grape could hear him sneer at them, she had always thought he must hate children, but she didn't realise how much until that moment.

Arty Grape waited for the perfect moment that she had been subconsciously thinking about thought about for weeks, it was the moment that she would slip past the cloaked man with deception and without detection. Arty Grape was extremely confident, there was no other way for her to be, but really she didn't know what she was doing--Let's be honest, do you know what you are doing?

Her moment would soon arrive. The seconds turned into minutes and her minutes into hours and she patiently waited. She watched the cloaked man walk backwards and forwards along his gantry. He turned towards her and looked directly at her, or at least in her direction, like he knew she was there, and then he abruptly looked away like she wasn't even there. This was Arty Grape's moment, she knew it would eventually come so she pounced upon it like a young child on a packet of sweets. The cloaked man was a creature of habit after all, she had found a weakness in his armour. Arty Grape had been watching him since she had arrived in the factory and she knew how he walked, she knew the amount of steps he took and she knew how his body would move. So she bolted silently on her hands and knees out of the tiny corridor, sticking to the wall as much she could. Arty Grape knew there would be another corridor waiting for her around the next corner, the corridor the cloaked man had walked down, she was going to find out where he had come from and what clues he had left. She moved quickly and quietly towards the next corridor, not stopping or looking at her surroundings until she was face to face with her next challenge. Arty Grape swung her body around the corner of the corridor and stopped to look, it was then that she faced a red door that stared back at her from the end of the white corridor. She had no time to think, she paused only for half a moment before running as fast as she could towards it, the cloaked man would turn soon and discover her. The corridor seemed to stretch forever as Arty Grape rushed down it towards the red door, as soon as it was within her grasp she lunged for the round golden door handle that was the last thing between her and security. But no matter how hard she pulled the golden handle, the door did not open

Of course it didn't.

Chapter Nineteen

I was only joking when I said the red door didn't open, sorry about that, I changed my mind. If the door didn't open then she would have been discovered by the cloaked man, and if she had been detected then this would be a very different story, involving torture and horrible things that exist in this world.

Arty Grape pulled the red door open and threw herself inside, the cloaked man hadn't heard her and he hadn't turned around. She quickly pulled the red door shut, concealing and trapping herself in the room behind the red door. She picked herself up and she stood staring at the red door, she realised she hadn't breathed properly for a few minutes and she needed to catch her breath. She gulped down as much air until she could breath properly again, without gasping for her life. Arty Grape began to take in the room she found herself in. The very first thing she noticed was the soft lush carpeted floor, its colour felt otherworldly when she gazed upon it and she felt like she was on the moon when she walked across it. She looked up to discover that the walls were painted black and no windows adorning any wall. In the middle of the room sat a small round table with a beautifully crafted wooden chair resting under it, it's legs were small but its back was tall, it looked like a modern throne for a king or queen to rule with an iron rod. On top of the table sat a small lamp that let off a golden glow, despite its size it was still able to illuminate. Arty Grape walked precariously towards the round table, as she walked the writing on the wall in the distance became clear.

Timo Mass said the writing on the wall.

Arty Grape had hoped to discover a one hundred page document detailing where she is, why she is and who is Timo Maas, the one executing a sick and twisted plan?

Arty Grape was scared, she didn't know what to do next, salvation had been removed from her, she was non the wiser and she found herself in a worse predicament than she was before. Arty Grape could only travel back the same way she had arrived, but she didn't know how she was going to do it-- Despite what you may think, she had meticulously planned her way to the room behind the red door, but she hadn't planned how to get out of it. It was hope that had brought her there, so she had no reason to plan her return journey, she thought all would be revealed upon her arrival.

Arty Grape didn't know what was waiting for her on the other side of the red door, that single thought made her panic and she began to struggle for air; her chest started to heave and she inhaled and exhaled too little of the precious air. Arty Grape couldn't catch her breath, so she decided the only logical thing to do was to hold it instead. Soon she stopped panicking and calm passed over her body, she was ready to try breathing again, never did she ever think she would forget how to breath.

Arty Grape started to focus her thoughts again, she thought about the predicament she found herself in. *How am I going to escape the room with the red door* she asked herself. She paced around the room, accepting any idea that came to her. The red door stared at her and she stared back at the red door, she had to face her next fear, she had to pass beyond its threshold once again. The red door became her nemesis, it wouldn't beat her, this wouldn't be her end. She walked to face the red door, and slowly she reached out and held its golden door knob, then she prepared to face the cloaked man. She knew there was no perfect moment to open the red door, she was blind to the other side, she grabbed the door knob harder and pushed it wide open as fast as she could. In the distance she could see the cloaked man on the walkway, she noticed that his cloak swooshed and swirled to the right, Arty Grape knew he had just turned around moments ago. This was her chance to run back to the spiral staircase and she wasn't going to wait for a second chance. Arty Grape dashed to the end of the corridor as fast as her legs would carry her. The cloaked man had eight more steps to take before he turned to discover one of the souls he had taken had freed themselve. Arty Grape ran and she ran until she reached the end of the corridor, she grabbed on to the corner of the wall with her finger tips and swung herself around it. The muscles in her fingers had never worked so hard before, they held on for dear life, her life; they turned red as the blood rushed to the tips of each finger. Arty Grape carried on running towards the spiral stair case, its twists and its turns would would take her back to the safety of her own room, a room that had become her prison, but now felt like home. Arty Grape flung herself into the small corridor led her to the spiral staircase, she flung herself to the ground, stopping in herself in her tracks. She was faced with the drying blood she had spilled the last time she was there. She gasped for every breath until she was ready to stand up again. Arty Grape didn't know if the cloaked man had seen her, she didn't have the time to stop and look. *If I had been spotted then I would find out soon enough* she thought. She sat on the spiral staircase that had delivered her to the seventh floor and she hid in its shadows until it was time for all the children to return to their rooms again. Hour after hour she sat there waiting, occasionally drifting of into a day dream, a dream in which she had awoken from her nightmare. She started to fall asleep whilst she rested her head in her hands, and the moment she began to fade into sleep she was abruptly interrupted by the sound of the children marching from their desks.

'It's Time!' spoke the voice.

The cloaked man walked back towards his empty room, Arty Grape heard each of his dirty steps as he moved. She wondered what he did there, she thought to herself that there must be more to the room behind the red door, she must have missed something. She continued to listen to his footsteps, she waited for them to become faint before she snuck down the spiral staircase to join the stream of children. She waited and she waited for the very last child and then she craftily joined the back of the queue until finding an empty room to occupy.

Finally she was back in her current comfort zone, pretending to pretend again. She sat on the edge of the bed and began to process all the things that had just happened, but nothing had happened, the only thing she had discovered were more unanswered questions. *Who is Timo Mass?* she thought. *If the cloaked man isn't Timo Maas then who is he?* She kept pondering. Arty Grape's mind couldn't escape the writing on the wall, every time she closed her eyes from that day forth, she would see the words burned to the back of her eyelids.

Timo Maas spoke the words.

Timo Maas

Look at me trying to trick you with the title of my chapters. This chapter isn't going to tell you who Timo Maas is, this is a different chapter altogether. I probably should have called it 'Something Different' because it has more to do with that than Timo Maas. Nevertheless, we shall talk about Timo Mass or will we be talking about the cloaked man? Lets join one of them in the empty room for a moment and see where that takes us.

The cloaked man stood in the room behind the red door, but he was in a very different room to what Arty Grape had found herself in. A very different room indeed. How had he conjured this magic trick nobody knew, but there he sat. His face was hidden by his own shadow as he paced backwards and forwards. His fingers twitched with every second step and he muttered to himself in his head. He sat down on a comfortable chair and he turned towards a gramophone resting on a round and beautifully crafted table. He placed a record onto its turntable and the gramophone began to crackle with love before the music began to bounce off the walls in the room. The cloaked man needed a moment to himself, he needed to think and reflect. He sat in his comfortable chair until the needle of gramophone reached the end of the record, only then did he release himself from his dark thoughts. He stood and walked to a large window in the room and gazed upon the town of Eden. The whole town had succumbed to his will, he knew he had it in the palm of his hands, but it wasn't enough, he needed to control the minds of the children too. They had been made to fear what he might do to them, but he knew he couldn't stop their inevitable dissent. He needed to figure out how he could consume and control every fibre of their being, and each day that he failed he became violently frustrated. The cloaked man gazed upon his reflection in the large window and smiled, he congratulated himself for being able to suppress his inner most demons of doubt, the doubt of knowing that what he was doing was wrong. In his fragmented mind he was a good person, he was loved by all around him and they worshiped and held him high. He wouldn't stop until all the children in the world realised he was there to save them, and worshipping him was the best thing they could do. He was a monster but it wasn't his fault, he hadn't been born a monster he had become a monster through the passing of time. The cloaked man had always been show the opposite of love, so it was inevitable for him to become who he was. He had locked himself away from the world for too long, he was becoming stranger and stranger. He sat staring at his reflection and, at the same time, the town of eden in the distance. His eyes glazed over as the music began to fill his head, it played over and over, one thousand and one times.

Oh, jeepers creepers, where'd ya get those peepers?
Jeepers creepers, where'd ya get those eyes?
Oh, gosh all, git up, how'd they get so lit up?
Gosh all, git up, how'd they get that size?

The music had laid a path that took him to the madness in his mind, when it played he became brainwashed just like the people in the town of Eden had, just like them he had no control over it, he couldn't escape what he had been programmed by the music to do, so he continued to torture the children in his very own and very special way.

'It's time.' spoke the voice.

'10233478344.' spoke the voice.

'Prepare.' spoke the voice.

He had forgotten who's voice it was that echoed through the factory, was it his voice he wondered, had he spoken those words . Every moment he had ever had had evaporated, he didn't know who he was and he didn't know how he had become the man he is today. He had grown paranoid of his own shadow, he could no longer trust his own instincts. Deeper and deeper he fell into the music that played. The beat hurt his eyes and terrible ideas swam around the inside of his head, ideas of how to dispose of the children once he had finished with them. He couldn't stop thinking evil thoughts, he couldn't block them out, he had stopped trying to deny them a long time ago, and he had hidden them well from others that had surrounded him in his previous life. The cloaked man stood up and began pace the room, his fingers twitched with every footstep, and he started to find it hard to concentrate, thousands of thoughts flooded his brain all at the same time, it was like entering into a warp speed of words and ideas. He stopped and looked up at the wall in front of him; '*Timo Maas*' said the words. He stared at them wondering who Timo Mass is or was. Who had wrote those words? Was he Timo Mass? Had he written his name there so he wouldn't forget himself?--Let's stop now shall we, let's think happy thoughts, lets' think about daisies and butterflies until we are blue in the face, let's not think about the awful things that I'm about to do to you, let's not think about the people I am watching as I write this, the people I am following and observing their every moment. Lets think of other things like daisies, butterflies and upside down rainbows.

The Third Day Is Coming.

Chapter Twenty One

Mr Fox sat at his desk and he began to notice something disturbing happening in the factory. He had noticed the number of grown ups watching him had decreased over the weeks and the days, but no he started to notice the opposite. They were returning in large numbers, he carefully glanced around the room and he could see that there was more of them then there were yesterday, and more than yesterdays yesterday too. Out of thin air they had seem to appear, it was as if they knew a defiance was rising, a defiance started by Arty Grape and Mr Fox. The children didn't want to live in fear anymore, they didn't want to be controlled, they had realied that if they did nothing, then nothing would ever change. Together the children would overcome the evil that had held them prisoners for far too long. Mr Fox had started to see the messages appear in the white pages that rested on each desk every day, and he started to write more and more messages to whoever was listening. Slowly over time hundreds upon hundreds of children were secretly communicating using the written and all powerful word. He wrote to his sister, hoping to find her in the white pages one day. The dissent of the children had started to happen and there was no stopping it now.

The days passed quicker than usual to Mr Fox and before

he know it the third day had arrived again. The last days of the factory had begun and there was very little time to prepare or muster up the courage the children needed to start their uprising. The messages of hope kept flooding through the factory, more and more of the children began to listen to the truth of their situation and awaken from their deep slumber.

At the end of each day Mr Fox returned to his uncomfortable bed and he would lay down and stare up at the ceiling, he wondered about being free again and what he would do with his freedom if it should ever return to him again. Would he lead a better life he thought, would he make more use of the endless time he thought he had. Mr Fox realised what he had come to miss the most during his incarceration, it was his loving parents and his ridiculous sister. He had forgotten what the gentle touch of their beings felt like. Could his parents be fixed he thought, would everything return to normal. As Mr Fox laid there and thought deeply about everything he heard the music begin to play through the air. The music always reminded him why he was there and it also reminded him why he needed to escape.

Jeepers Creepers, Where'd ya Get Those Eyes....

Mr Fox knew the music had everything to do with everything, but he didn't know how or more importantly why. He sat on his bed night after night thinking about the *why of why* everything was happening but he found never came to an understanding.

Another day passed and Mr Fox found himself laying on his bed, again, and staring into his own thoughts.

'Sleep.' spoke the voice and the lights immediately shut off. He thought that something didn't quite feel right, the lights had never turned off that quickly for a long time he thought but soon after that thought he was asleep. He had no choice but to sleep, he had been conditioned just like an animal to obey.

Mr Fox began to slowly drift into his dreams, they were like the waves in the sea, coming and going as they pleased but bringing different things to the shore of his mind each time. He could hear the voices of the angels singing in the music that played, he could hear the muttering voices of his mama and papa. Mr Fox was home. He got out of his bed and he put his monster feet slippers and went upstairs, walking past his mama and papa's room, he noticed they had left their bed messy like they always had done. He past his sisters room, she had fallen asleep with her door wide open and he could see her laying in her bed with a smile on her face. His sister was having a wonderful dream inside the dream of Mr Fox's. *Who knows what she's dreaming* thought Mr Fox. He had passed the point of knowing if he was dreaming too, and everything felt as real to him as real could be. He stopped to look at her for a few moments more, he realised how much she annoyed him but how much he loved her too and then he continued to conjure her dreams. He walked upstairs to the kitchen and found that nobody was there, the kettle was boiling on the worktop, he waited for the switch to click and the water to stop boiling but it never did. The smell of bread had disappeared and the muttering voices had gone. He walked into the living room expecting to find his mama and papa sitting talking on the sofa, putting the world right with their opinions, but instead he found that his imagination had sprayed words on the wall. *'Timo Maas'* said the letters. He stared at the words for a moment but he couldn't decipher their meaning, his thoughts were soon interrupted with the sound of the doorbell. He left the room and went to answer the door but before he could reach the door it opened and Mr Fox discovered there was another world out there. The closer he drew to the door the more things he could see. On the other side of the door he saw himself sleeping, in his room, in the factory on the hill. He walked through the door and towards his himself, he looked at himself, before he climbed into himself, and that is where he found himself when he woke up the next day. Mr Fox opened his eyes and he felt refreshed, he felt good, he felt elated, a feeling he hadn't experienced for a very long time; He awoke feeling like things were going to change.

Mr Fox had seen the writing on the wall in the red room.

Chapter Twenty Two

The third had day arrived. The children didn't know it but it would be the last third day that they would ever see and They were also unaware that every day the factory had become fortified with more of the parents living in their altered state. Escape would soon become a ridiculous myth and freedom would forever be out of their reach.

Arty Grape and Mr Fox rose from their slumber that day feeling strong, positive and ready. They knew they would leave the factory today, they had woken up and had the same thoughts, like they were connected some how and nothing was going to stop them. Arty Grape opened her eyes and then Mr Fox opened his eyes. They both waited for three for the last time. They door appeared in their room and they stepped on to the walkway to face all the other children, hoping they would follow them when the time came. They marched to a desk and they ate their disgusting breakfast along the way before they sat down and didn't follow their daily orders. They sat and they didn't life a finger or one of the white pages, the children stared up high towards the seventh floor. Everyone could feel a strange silence in the air, the children didn't move and the guards didn't know what to do, they had never seen such mass disobedience before. They stared at the children, but still they did nothing, it was as if they had now become the ones who were afraid, the ones that would have their own truth reversed on them. Every child sat patiently and waited for the cloaked man to make his appearance. They watched the large clock on the wall tick the time away until the seconds turned into multiple minutes. Arty Grape's palms started to get sweaty and Mr Fox's brow began to perspire, their nerves were tested, it was something thing they had never experienced before. Every child felt that things were about to change but they didn't know whether it was for the good, the good that the fairy stories had told them about. The clock kept ticking, it was fast approaching the point on the clock where the cloaked man would usually appear. Tick, tick, tick went the clock and with every tick Arty Grape's palms sweated some more. Tick tick tick went the clock as Mr Fox wiped his brow with every second that evaporated. Tick, tick, tick went the clock until the cloaked man finally appeared. Arty Grape gazed upon him with the same disgust he had shown her. She wanted to destroy him, like he had slowly destroyed her, she wanted to find out who he was and why he was doing such evil things to her and all the other children. He paced the floor more intently than on all the other days, you could sense the anger building in him as he looked down upon the children. He could feel their obedience starting to slip, but he had no idea how much. He stopped walking, turning towards them, he looked at all their faces to see who they were and what they were doing. The children had always been completely irrelevant to the him for such a long time, but today they were no longer irrelevant, they were about to matter to him and to themselves. The cloaked man was about to find out how much he had underestimated the children, they were capable of so much more than he had thought or ever planned for.

He looked and looked at the children beneath him and he could sense they were no longer scared of him, they had each other, they stood together for the first time and he could sense an uprising in their little souls.

Arty Grape looked up fiercely at the cloaked man, she was waiting to catch his eye, she wanted to look at him deeper than any person had ever looked at him before. He paced back and forth for a again for a few moments longer before stopping to stare at his accomplishment that would soon be taken away from him. It was then that he caught Arty Grapes stare; it was then that Arty Grape looked deep into his eyes from afar. That moment was the start of her first stand, she kept her gaze tightly on him and the cloaked man returned it back to her. Arty Grape wasn't backing down, she would let blood pour from her eyes before she looked away. Arty Grape rose from her chair and stood tall, and her brother immediately spotted her a few rows ahead. He was overcome with emotions and he had to compose himself, he knew if he didn't tears would burst from his eyes. Everything around him ceased to exist, even time itself didn't tick or tock. He watched Arty Grape step out from behind her desk, she did it with confidence and grace, all fear had left her body. She was about to change her fate and the fate of everyone around her. She had come to realise that there was no fate worse than the factory on the hill.

Arty Grape stood by the side of her desk, waiting and hoping for all the other children to make a stand with her too.

Mr Fox's palms began to sweat and a panic consumed his body, he didn't know what he was going to do, he didn't know how things were going to turn out, he became afraid and suddenly he felt responsible all the children around him; but he knew what he needed to do. Mr Fox needed to join his sister and, without a moments hesitation he pushed his chair back, the noise echoed through the silent factory, and abruptly stood tall with his sister, he wanted to show the other children that they were not alone.

The cloaked man couldn't believe what he was seeing and the minions that surrounded him didn't know what to do either. The cloaked man stared at Arty Grape and his gaze was only broken when he saw Mr Fox stand from behind his desk. Soon he didn't know where to look, one by one hundreds of children began to stand, each and everyone of them staring at him standing high on the seventh floor. The children didn't know what was coming next, they merely exercised faith in something they couldn't see.

Arty Grape watched more and more of the children rise from their seats, and her confidence started to grow, like a tree from the smallest of seeds. Arty Grape was ready to make her next move, she was ready to take her hand off the chess piece. She ran through the rows of tables and chairs, speeding towards the spiral staircase that would lead her to the seventh floor once again, to face her captor for the first and final time.

'Arty' shouted Mr Fox, stopping her in her speedy tracks, turning to look for her brother's voice. It was as if she sensed where he was, she saw him immediately in the sea of children that surrounded her; a huge smile erupted upon her face and for and instant moment she forgot what she was about to do and stopped to smile at her brother, the light beamed from her beautiful white teeth and her green eyes, she shone like a beacon of hope in Mr Fox's story of things.

'Wait!' Mr Fox shouted as he ran towards his sister. They would finish their journey through the factory on the hill together. He ran towards her and they both leapt into each other's arms, holding on to the other as tightly as they could, but there was no time to waste.

'Where are you going Arty?' he asked.

'I'm going to the seventh floor.' she replied.

'The seventh floor? I'm coming with you.', and just like that they were gone.

Their sights were set on the seventh floor and Arty Grape's sights were set on the cloaked man, he would not escape, he would answer for everything. The other children ran around the factory like wild animals, throwing themselves like wild beasts on to anyone that stood it their way, the walls of Jericho had already be stormed and the horns had stopped playing.

'This way!' Arty Grape bellowed. 'This way, follow me!' as she headed to the spiral staircase. Mr Fox followed his sister and some of the children followed him, he was their temporary leader, just like Arty Grape was his They traversed the stairs to the seventh floor and Arty Grape led them straight to the red door. There was nowhere for the cloaked man to hide anymore, he was about to face her and them, they would become the judge and the jury, his verdict had already been determined, before his story had been heard. The red door grew bigger and bigger as she ran towards it, but she was no longer frightened by what she would find behind it. Arty Grape reached for the golden door knob for the third time and pulled it open, she stormed inside to find a room she had already found herself in, there was no signs of the cloaked man that she had hoped to find. *This is impossible* she thought. The cloaked man wasn't a magician so how had he performed his trick. The writing on the wall had gone; the name *Timo Maas* had been erased from the wall, like it had been erased from history or at least Arty Grape's history. The suffering that Arty Grape and all the children had endured needed to be answered for, they were going to find him, they were going to make him pay in whatever currency they could create for his crimes.

'What do we do now?' asked Mr Fox.

'We find a way out of this place.' she angrily replied.

Arty Grape needed some time to think, she needed some time to allow the ideas to bubble to her surface.

* * *

'It's time.' spoke the voice.

Chapter Twenty Three

The children roamed the corridors, some followed others and others followed some. They couldn't find the exit to the factory on the hill, they were still trapped, no matter how hard they tried there seemed be no way out of the hell they had found themselves in. The main doors where all the children had been led through on arrival had been sealed tight, signs had been bolted to the door that said 'Thou children shalt not pass'.

Arty Grape and Mr Fox had no choice but to leave the room behind the red door. They roamed the huge expanse of the factory on the hill, looking for any clues they could find. The factory was a Chinese puzzle that needed to be solved, a puzzle that would eventually release them back into the world. No matter how hard the children tried, they found nothing, not a single thing led them to their freedom. The children never gave up, they went up, and then down and then they went over there, before eventually realising they were going nowhere fast. *Where had he gone?*--Where had the cloaked man gone?

Arty Grape could find no secret passages, she could find no hidden levers to pull and the cloaked man still eluded her every idea. *Where has he gone?* She thought again before deciding to go back to the red door and into the room that lay behind it.

'Fox. Come with me, I have an idea.'

'What is it?'

'Just follow me to the red door and I'll show you.'

'Again Arty. We've been back there at least seven times, there's nothing there, he's not there, he's gone, we're not going to find anything.'

'Just follow me, please Fox! I'm going to try something different this time.' As they headed towards the red door, it felt like they had to swim their way through a sea of children that roamed the floors of the factory. They climbed the spiral staircase again and they worked their way down the long white corridor towards the red door. The door had become the bane of Arty Grape's existence; her gut feeling told her that she had missed something vital, instead of listening to what her thoughts were telling her, she was following her feelings.

'What's your new idea then Arty?'

'I'll show you.'

Arty Grape reached out to the golden door knob on the red door, her eyes looked as cold as steel as she stared down the door like it was another human being standing in her way. She turned the golden door knob, closing her eyes as she heard the mechanism unlock, she paused for a moment and wondered if her new idea would disappoint.

'What are you waiting for?' asked Mr Fox but Arty Grape didn't answer him, instead she just stood there silently with her eyes closed breathing so deeply her brother could see her chest pump up and down. *Nothing is what it seems* she thought and when that thought had finished she pushed the door, instead of pulling it, it was the only idea that she had left in her head, so she pushed the door open, keeping her eyes firmly shut. With each step she took into the room behind the red door, she opened her eyelids a millimetre at a time. Mr Fox hadn't realised that his sister had pushed instead of pulled, it was an insignificant detail to him.

To each of their surprise and to the hope of Arty Grape, they found themselves in a very different room. The first thing to strike them was the daylight that streamed into it, it struck their eyes and sizzled their retinas, they were blinded by its beautiful power, they had forgotten about the light until it hit them once again. Slowly their eyes adjusted and they wiped away what felt like blood from their eyes, but it was only the tears that the pure sunlight had forced from their tear ducts. When their vision returned they saw a large window in the room, it looked down upon the entirety of the town of Eden. They walked towards the large window and stood inches away from the glass, staring at the sun high in the sky; they kept watching it until it slowly fel behind the hills in the distance. They became mesmerised by the colour of the sky that began to fade from the day and travelled into the night. Gazing upon the beauty of the sun setting calmed them, they didn't really know what stress was but they could feel it leaving every muscle and every bone in their bodies.

'I'd forgotten what the sun looked like.' one of them said.

'I'd forgotten about the colour blue.' said the other.

They watched the sun slowly leave them for another day; they knew it would return again on the morrow, they knew the sun would never let them down--at least not for a long time.

Mr Fox noticed a clicking sound that had always been there but had failed to notice.

'Can you hear that Arty?' he said as he continued to gaze at the remnants of the sun falling behind the hill in the distance. Arty Grape's brain started to tune into the clicking sound too, and they both simultaneously turned their heads towards the noise, which was coming from behind them, in a dark corner of the room. As their heads turned their eyes began to slowly absorb the rest of the room. Mr Fox noticed that the walls were black and covered with words written in chalk, the words made no sense to him, they were clearly the ramblings of a mad man he thought. Arty Grape noticed the writing on the walls, but to her it made complete sense. Arty Grape was after all the product of a mad man who had shaped her into what he wanted her to be and what he wanted her to see.

In the far corner of the round room sat a gramophone on a table, its needle had reached the end of a record that it had enjoyed playing and instead of returning to its home it kept trying to find the next track on the record to follow. The clicking sound travelled through the horn of the gramophone, getting louder and louder as it moved. Mr Fox walked towards the musical contraption, picked up the arm of the needle and put it back whence it came.

Arty Grape and Mr Fox eradicated the clicking sound, which meant they could concentrate on the intricate detail of the gramophone; it was a beautiful piece of equipment and upon further inspection they could see it was connected to an innumerable amount of different coloured cables. Arty Grape pulled on one of the cables and attempted to trace where it had come from. The cable weaved and weaved into a cleverly disguised room that Arty Grape and Mr Fox had failed to see. Inside the hidden room they found a multitude of computers, the lights of each computer flashed a different colour every other second. The machines looked like they were trying to communicate with each other in a language that only binary people could understand. Arty Grape and Mr Fox stared at the wall of computers buzzing away, unbeknown to them the arm of the gramophone lifted, and it began to make itself to the beginning of the record once again; the needle rested its weary head upon the vinyl tracks beneath it and the music began to play.

Oh jeepers creepers, where'd ya get those peepers?

Jeepers creepers, where'd ya get those eyes?
Oh, gosh all, git up, how'd they get so lit up?
Gosh all, git up, how'd they get that size?

Arty Grape and Mr Fox heard the music play and then they looked at each other. They knew immediately what they needed to do, they needed to destroy the music, they knew it was the music that had caused all their suffering in the town of Eden.

'We need to destroy the music Fox.' Her brother didn't need to be persuaded, he wanted to destroy the music as much as she did, the music had controlled things for far too long and it was time to bring it to an end. They followed the cables along the floor and then they began to pull on every red, green, yellow or black cable they could lay their hands on. They had turned into the animals that they had never wanted to become, but always knew they were. Arty Grape and Mr Fox had become lost in the moment and they didn't stop until their task of destruction was complete. *Before you create, you destroy* flowed through Arty Grape's mind, her art teacher had said it to her one day, but that day was eight hundred and sixty five days ago she thought before thinking how strange thoughts are, the things you can't control popping into existence. Mr Fox kept pulling until there were no more cables left to pull, he and his sister had ripped out every connection and the music stopped playing and the air was clean again.

Mr Fox walked back towards the gramophone, he used all his strength to pick it up from where it sat and he held it high above his head; at that moment he was the world's strongest man, his biceps bulged and his face looked like it was about to explode before his legs quivered under its weight. He launched the contraption across the room with the last of his might, the gramophone bounced off the wall and onto the floor like it was a rubber ball, he felt disappointed that it didn't smash into one thousand pieces, like a fragile wine glass, it was as if it couldn't be destroyed--It couldn't be destroyed, and it would play its filthy music on other days to come.

'This is pointless.' Arty Grape said.

'Yip.' panted Mr Fox.

'At least the music has stopped playing. Okay....' Arty Grape walked back into the room with the computers and looked at the cables that carpeted the floor. One cable in particular stood out to her, a thick cable that had the plastic skin of a serpent, but the colours of an African Zebra. Arty Grape slowly pulled it through her hands until she couldn't pull it anymore, and when she couldn't pull it anymore, she pulled even harder. Arty Grape became like a cannibal that had been fed fresh human meat, she was ravenous and she wouldn't stop until the cable had been torn from its home, just like an arm from a rotting socket. She tore cable after cable from wherever they were plugged in to, she didn't know, she didn't care. When she tired of her task, she picked up one of the mazillion computers and threw it as hard as she could at the wall, screaming like an animal as it flew through the air before crashing towards the ground. Arty Grape didn't know her own strength and the destruction had begun, Her animal instincts had been drawn closer to the surface, she had been pushed too far during her stay at the factory on the hill and the monster she kept hidden burst into rage. Arty Grape had never experienced rage before, it was like she was filled with rocket fuel that had been discovered under the ground and accidentally ignited by a fool with a match.

Mr Fox hadn't noticed his sister disappearing, but he heard a disturbance in the room with the computers and he knew exactly what she was doing. He joined his sister and picked up any computer he could lay his hands upon and began to throw as many of the hideous machines at the walls with all his tiny strength, some of them exploded into several pieces, others fell to the floor without making a sound. The lights on the computers they destroyed no longer communicated any ones or zeros to each other, they were disconnected from the electronic underworld, cut off from the rest of the civilization of ones and zeros.

Arty Grape's and Mr Fox's rage began to fade, like most human beings, they only had so much spirit inside them. The last computer flew through the air and smashed into the unforgiving walls, every little piece of energy they had left in their souls had been depleted, even despair had left them. Adrenaline coursed through their veins and their hands shook uncontrollably in front of the very eyes that had never lied to them before. Arty Grape looked at her brother, she felt like she had failed him, she felt like they would be forever stuck in the factory on the hill. She had to stop herself from crying as a wave of emotion swept over her, but she wasn't finished yet, she would not be defeated and her determination would carry her forth.

They had destroyed everything in sight, but they were still with no place to go. Arty Grape walked back to the large window that looked out into the world and over the town of Eden, the window was the only place in the factory that allowed the light to breathe. They stood looking out of the large window and their thoughts turned to Eden as they gazed down upon it. They looked at the town and hoped that they would live happily ever after, just like all the other fairy stories that they had read, but this wasn't a fairy story and it hadn't been for a very long time, this was the real world that they had been forced to face, and it was hideous and horrible, but they had survived and would forever be changed.

Arty Grape and Mr Fox still hadn't found the evil that had taken them to the factory on the hill and they didn't know how long that evil would lurk in the backgrounds of their minds. It would become yet another demon they needed to expel, another thing they needed to bury deep down and forget if they were to ever have a normal happily ever after life. The people of Eden had become used to the strange things that occurred under the blanket of its stars and Arty Grape and Mr Fox were beginning to see the strangeness too – As shall you.

Memories of the factory began to flood back to her, she had been there before on many different occasions, and in different times. The factory would look different every time and it always served a different purpose, but it was always the same place disguised as something else. Arty Grape had been a visitor of the factory on the hill in her dreams, but for the first time she realised they may not have been dreams, they were remnants of her past experiences that had been forgotten over time or removed because they were too painful to remember; she didn't know which was which or what was when but she finally realised the factory was no stranger to her and she would be brought here once again, if she were ever to leave.

Arty Grape and Mr Fox continued to stare out of the large window, both of them silently thinking of how to escape their fate.

'We need to get home Fox. We need to leave this place.'

'How?' he asked.

'I don't know, but we'll figure it out. We always figure it out Fox.'

They looked around the room trying to find any sign that led them in the direction of their freedom, but they couldn't see an entrance or an exit. They checked the floors for secret passages and ran their hands across the walls to feel for any cracks that may have revealed the light to the world outside, but they found nothing. Arty Grape and Mr Fox had exhausted every possibility in the room behind the red door.

There were no answers to the world they found themselves in, only more questions which nobody could explain. *Who is the cloaked man?* Arty Grape thought. *Why have we been punished?* Mr Fox thought.--These are the answers that you and I will never find out, not in this story or any other story, sometimes there are no answers.

It was time to leave the room behind the red door, they made their way back to the main hall, climbing down the cold spiral staircase, they were greeted by the other children running around like headless chickens. Every child was trying to find a way out of the mess that been created for them. The children were all moving in a different directions, it was a ridiculous sight to see. All they needed to do was to work together, it just took them time to realise that, but by that time it was already too late, panic and selfishness had already set in, it was every child for themselves.

'There has to be a way out Fox.' Arty Grape shouted to her borther amongst the chaos.

'Where did the cloaked man go Arty.' Mr Fox furiously wondered.--I hope and I'm also sure you're all wondering where the cloaked man went too, aren't you? If I tell you, do you promise not to tell Arty Grape and Mr Fox, do you promise to keep this secret forever?

Arty Grape and Mr Fox ran around the factory floor, bumping into the children that were lost amongst themselves. They didn't know what to do, they knew there must be something they had missed, something they foolishly forgot to think of, something that would come to them very soon and lead the way. Arty Grape ran around the factory and Mr Fox followed her, even though he knew she didn't know where she was going. They ran up and they ran down the expanse of the factory, but it was no use, there was nowhere to go and nothing revealed itself to them. Arty Grape sat in one of the chairs she had sat in every day whilst she worked through the white pages, hundreds of children ran around her as she laid her head on the table, there was nothing left for her to do. She sat there for far too long feeling hopeless before she sat up and screamed. 'Aaaaaaaaaaaaaaaaaaaaaaaaaaaaaaaaaaaaaaaaaaaah.' she blasted into the ceiling of the factory, but her screams could barely be heard amongst the hustle and bustle of the other helpless children.

'Are you okay Arty?' asked Mr Fox, but he received no answer. 'Are you okay?' he asked again. Arty Grape took a moment before turning her head to look at him.

'We need to go back to the room behind the red door.' She didn't even think to wait for her brother, she stood up from the desk and made her way to the room that had perplexed her. Mr Fox followed her and after they had pushed their way past through the debris of children they stood outside the red door once again. Arty Grape entered the room, just like she had before, and stared at the large window displaying its beautiful view. Arty Grape could have stood there for the rest of her days but she knew she had an impossible mission to complete. She stared at the beautiful vista for a few minutes more before turning to the gramophone on the floor, Mr Fox watched her slowly but carefully carry the contraption towards the window, and then he watched her hurl it towards the glass that was the only barrier between them and the free air on the other side. It was the only weakness in the fortress of the factory that she could find. The gramaphone bounced off the glass, leaving the smallest of marks, and then it bounced across the floor, but that didn't deter her. They both continued to throw whatever they could find at the window, it was their only hope of leaving the factory. The glass seemed impenetrable but they would not give up. Whatever they could find they threw at it, each time with more force, waiting for a sign the window was weakening.

'There's a crack Fox, is that a crack?' she excitedly shouted at her brother. Mr Fox walked to where his sister was pointing and examined what he thought she could see.

'It's definitely a crack.' he smiled before throwing another computer at the window.

'Keep throwing things at that crack.' Arty Grape demanded. Mr Fox agreed and they both threw machine after machine until the crack in the glass grew like a spiders' web until the window couldn't take anymore, and the only thing left for it to do was to explode in defeat. Arty Grape and Mr Fox had beaten the window, they had removed the barrier between them and the world that awaited them. The air flooded and filled their nostrils and sweet memories were forged into their thoughts. They were one step closer to a future that didn't involve the factory on the hill, but what that future would hold neither of them knew.

Chapter Twenty Four

ARE THERE STILL ADULTS IN THE FACTORY

Arty Grape and Mr Fox breathed in the fresh air that flowed cross the landscape and into the factory on the hill, it was cool, crisp and comforting, they could even taste its sweetness as it filled their bodies. Pieces of glass large and small to the floor, whilst other shards of glass clung to the metal window frame for dear life, not wanting to admit defeat, not wanting to let go.

Arty Grape and Mr Fox waited until it was safe to step closer to the edge of the shattered window, carefully stepping over any bits of broken glass as they moved forward to see what lay ahead of them. As they stood at the edge of the factory Mr Fox reached for his sisters hand and he held it tight. Their journey wasn't over, their journey had merely just begun and Mr Fox felt a comfort in knowing he would be doing it with his sister by his side. They peered over the window frame to discover the ground was a million miles away, they had no idea how they were going to get down, but down was the only option they had at that moment in time. They leant further forward and looked to their right, sitting close to the side of the building was a large tree, its branches stretched out like fingers and it caressed the air as the wind gently moved it.

'Maybe we can jump to that tree and climb down.' said Mr Fox.

'Are you kidding me!' Arty Grape immediately shouted back. 'It's too far, we'll never make it.'

'I can make it and if I can make it you can. Trust me.'

'There's no way you can make it Fox, no way.'

'I can make it. I know I can.' Mr Fox examined the tree intently, his head moved up and down and side to side, it was like he was trying to escape a paper maze with a pen. 'If I jump to that branch there, I can make it down to that branch and then that branch and then there.' He said, pointing to parts of the tree.

'One. I have no idea what you're pointing at and two you can't make it.'

'I can make it. What other choice do we have, do you have any other suggestions? This place is like a fortress locked from the outside.' Arty Grape started to look around the room for anything she could use or for any secrets she might have missed, but still nothing revealed itself to her.

'There must something that we're not seeing, something that we've...' before she could finish her sentence her foolish brother ran hard towards the window and leapt towards the tree. As he jumped through the air his legs still continued to move as if they were still in contact with the floor, his arms swung as they propelled him through the air and Arty's Grapes heart stopped beating as she watched in disbelief at what her idiot brother was attempting to do.

'Foooooooooox.' she screamed as she reached out for him. He disappeared out of her sight momentarily as he flew towards the sturdy tree, Arty Grape had no idea what fate he had met as she ran towards the window, praying that she wouldn't see him plummeting to his demise.

As the branches on the tree were within his reach he threw

his arms out with all the hope in his world, pleading with all the gods that existed to help him with his foolish endeavour. Mr Fox slammed hard into one of the ancient branches, his ribs creaked but they did not crack and he experienced pain like he had never experienced before, but he was alive at least he thought. He had winded himself and was struggling to breath as he held on tightly as his legs dangled and swayed in the wind.

'Fox. Fox. Are you okay? Fox!' Arty Grape shouted from the factory on the hill. Mr Fox still couldn't answer, he was trying to find the breath that the thick branches had knocked out of him. As he slowly filled his crushed lungs with oxygen the ability to speak returned to him and he eventually answered his sister in a breathless voice.

'I'm okay Arty. I'm okay.' he wheezed.

He held on tightly to the tree, hugging it like his life depended on it, which it did. He tried to feel for any branch he could beneath him.

'There's a branch below you Fox. It's below you and just in front of you. Feel with it with your legs.'

'What do you think I'm trying to do.' he wheezed to himself. He used his feet to carefully find a branch underneath him and then steadied himself before pulling himself up to sit carefully in the tree. He felt relieved, he had escaped the clutches of the factory, all that was left was for his sister to do the same thing.

'It's your turn now Arty.' he shouted. Arty Grape looked down and around.

'There's no way I can do it.' she shouted back.

'Yes you can. You're always saying how much better you are than me at everything. I don't like to admit it but you've always been able to jump further than me. You can do it, I know you can.

'Aaaaaaaaw Maaaaaaaaaan' Arty Grape said to herself. 'If I

die, I'm going to kill you.'

'You'll be fine. You can do it. Take a run up.' Arty Grape looked at the tree and looked at the ground, then she repeated that process a few more times before letting out a sigh of acceptance. It was the only way she would be able to escape the factory, she knew what needed to be done; she needed to risk her life to get it back. She walked away from the window, clearing anything that might be in her path that would affect her ridiculous attempt at throwing herself out of a window. She took a few moments to compose herself. 'Aim for that branch there.' Mr Fox said, pointing to the same branch he had smashed into. Arty Grape didn't respond, she knew which branch she was aiming for, all she needed to do now was to compose herself and ignore any doubt she had in her head. She took deeper and deeper breaths whilst staring at the gap between the window and the tree, it was now an enemy that had to be defeated, there was no option other than victory. Arty Grape was composed and ready for the challenge she had foolishly chosen to accept, because she had no choice. She told herself that once she commenced the countdown from 'three' there would be no turning back, so she prepared herself and looked one last time at the gap in the world between her prison and her freedom. Three, two, one counted the voices in her head and then she launched herself like a rocket towards the tree. As she reached the edge of existence, shards of glass fell from the window frame narrowly missing her, but she was undeterred, she was focused, nothing would distract her. She waited until the very last moment before she leapt as high as she could, her foot was half in the factory and half out transferring her kinetic energy into as much potential energy, and potential, as possible. Her body flew through the air with only one aim in sight, she jumped as high and as far as was humanly possible and she reached with all her life for the branches that would save her from her doom. Mr Fox could see the determination on her face as she glided through the cool air. Arty Grape hit the tree just as hard as Mr Fox had hit it, the force knocked the wind out of her just like it did to her brother, but at least she had her brother to grab her and stop her from falling. 'It's okay Arty. I've got you. I've got you now.' She held on tight to the thick branch and Mr Fox held on tightly to her, he could see her face grimacing with pain but it didn't matter, she was safe, she had finally escaped the factory on the hill, and she would never go back, she would never allow herself to be taken there again.

Chapter Twenty Five

Arty Grape and Mr Fox sat in the tree looking down at the
ground and planned how they would lay their tired feet once
again on the earth beneath them. They looked down through
the branches and gazed beyond the leaves wondering how
they would traverse the next part of their journey.

'What now Fox?' asked Arty Grape.

'Follow me. I think I can get us down.' he said confidently.
Mr Fox carefully shimmied across the thick branch he had all
of a sudden found himself on, he moved inch by inch,
holding on to the branches above with great care. He
shimmied until he could shimmy no more, then he
precariously felt for the branch below him with his toes as if
they had now become his fingers. When he felt it was safe he
stepped down on to the branch below. Arty Grape followed
him, stepping into each of the steps he had taken, not
wanting to stray from her brothers' path. She kept following
in his footsteps but then his trail stopped. They had climbed
down as far as they could, if they were to reach the ground
they would have to jump.

'What now Fox?' she questioned once again. 'We're still too
high up to jump.'

They were still at least fifty feet from the ground, but to
them it could have been one hundred thousand. Jumping

would certainly cause them a certain amount of pain that nobody would want to endure.

'Give me a minute to think.' he said as he frantically looked for an idea amongst the branches. He clearly didn't know what to do apart from jump, he hadn't thought this far ahead, ultimately it didn't matter to him; he would rather be stuck in a tree with his sister than stuck in the factory without her.

'How abo....'

'I've got it!' he said interrupting Arty Grape. 'If we both hang on to this branch and work our way towards the end, our weight will bend the branch and we'll be closer to the ground.'

'Seriously. That's your plan?'

'It is. Do you have a better one?' Arty Grape thought for a little before answering. 'No. I suppose it's not a bad plan. I just wish I didn't have to hang off a tree branch like some kind of ninja warrior.'

'Don't worry. It'll be fine.' he replied without even knowing if he was lying or telling the truth.

They carefully stepped further along the branch until it started to bend and bend and then bend some more. Mr Fox stopped to look down again at the floor they were desperate to stand upon. 'Okay, lets climb down and hang on. We'll climb down, hang and move across, do it as slowly as you can.' he calmly said, trying to convince his sister it was as normal as making a cup of tea. Luckily for them their papa had loved climbing trees and had passed his love over to them, even though they were afraid they were quietly confident.

'Alright, lets do it' said Arty Grape ',but can you move as quickly as you can, I'm not sure how long I can hold on for. If I can't hold on I'm not going to be able to climb back up.'

'Okay. I'll move as fast as I can.' replied Mr Fox.

They both sat down on the branch, grabbing whatever they

could to stabilise themselves. Mr Fox slowly lowered himself down until he was hanging from the tree, his arms could barely hold his own weight, there was nothing between him and the ground apart from the pain that awaited him should he fall. He swung his arms one at a time across the branch of the tree and Arty did her best keeping up with him, her arms burned inside, it felt like acid was coursing through her muscles. She wanted to tell her brother about the pain in her arms but she thought it would waste the energy she needed to finish the task she had set herself, Arty Grape needed reassurance that her brother felt the same.

'Aaaaaah. My arms are burning!' shouted Mr Fox as he moved. 'Keep going Arty, I can feel the branch bending.' He was right, the large branch had started to bend the further they moved, slowly they were inching their way towards the floor but it still looked like they were a mile away.

'I'm not sure how much longer I can hold on.' said Arty Grape.

'Keep going Arty. Keep going. It's bending.' They moved along the tree branch until it became too thin to move any further and Mr Fox thought it would surely snap if he continued. They hung there, stranded, with nowhere to go but down. The gap between them and the floor had decreased but they were still twenty feet from safety.

'What do we do now Fox?' Arty Grape calmly asked, knowing full well there was only one thing they could do, yet she still lived in hope that there was an alternative.

'The only thing we can do. Drop to the floor.' he replied. 'When you hit the floor roll, like we've been taught to roll. Make sure you roll straight away.' They kept hanging on, neither of them wanted face the pain that might come next.

'Shall I count to three Arty and then we let go?' asked Mr Fox. But before he could make that decision the tree decided for them. The branch began to creak and then crack and before they knew it, it had snapped and they plummeted to the floor hitting it like a dead weight, collapsing into a heap, their knees buckled underneath them and the pain escalated through their bones until it hit every nerve centre that was directly linked to their brain..

'Aaaaaaaagh' said Arty Grape.

'Aaaaaaaagh' said Mr Fox. They both lay on the ground holding their legs, waiting for the pain to end. They rived in agony until the pain became bareable, neither of them knew what was waiting for them when they tried to stand. Arty Grape looked over at Fox hoping he felt the same amount of pain that she did.

'Are you okay Fox?' Mr Fox grimaced before telling his sister he was fine.

'We've forgotten something Fox.'

'What do you mean?'

'We've forgotten about everyone else.'

'Ooooh. I forgot about them too. What should we do?' he asked.

'I'm not sure. We can't go back now. I think we should head home and see if we can find some help.'

'Okay.'

Arty Grape and Mr Fox stood up and then Mr Fox let out a huge scream. 'What's the matter Fox?' asked Arty.

'My knee, I've got a huge pain in my knee. Hold on.' Mr Fox put a little bit of weight on his knee. 'Aaaaaaaaah.' he screamed. 'I can't stand on my knee.'

'Okay. Shall we wait a minute, see if it gets better?'

'I don't think this is going to get better by waiting. I'm not staying here by myself, so if you can help me, we'll keep going?'

'Okay. Put your arm around me and I'll help you walk.' Arty Grape stepped towards her brother, stooped down and took his arm over her shoulder, supporting him with every step they made back to the town of Eden. It felt like they had walked for miles but with Mr Fox's injury, in reality, they had walked less than a mile. They looked back to survey the distance they had travelled and they could still see the factory on the hill. It shimmered at them, blinding their eyes as they stared at it. When they had approached the factory it emanated a darkness like that of a black hole, but as they left it, the factory had begun to glow.

'Do you know where we are Fox?' Arty Grape asked. Mr Fox pointed to the road they were walking towards. 'I think, we're at the top of the mountain behind our house. I think I remember driving down that road with papa before. I think I remember driving past this factory once upon a time.'

'Let's follow the road that way then.' said Arty Grape. So they continued to walk across the mountain terrain towards the gravely road until they had to make another decision. The air had started to get cold and the wind began to feel like another friend by their side keeping them company as they aimlessly wandered. 'C'mon Arty, this way.' shouted Mr Fox. Arty Grape had become lost in the landscape around her, she watched the sheep roam wild, some followed each other like lemmings and others paid no interest whilst they munched on the grassy mountain.

'Where are we going Fox? What are we doing? The only place we can go is home and we don't know what's there anymore.'

'It's the only place we can go.' he said.

'But what if....' Arty Grape didn't even want to finish her own sentence, the thought of it made shivers travel down her spine so she carried on walking without wanting to end her sentence. They continued to walk along the mountain road where the land stretched forever in each direction, they dragged their tired bodies step by step, the wind howled and the sun shone down on them in a hard and unforgiving manner, like a disapproving parent beating them down bit by bit. Arty Grape and Mr Fox reached a fork in the road and without thinking they turned right and followed the mountain road that passed through the trees that covered the road in darkness. Slowly the light began to fade away as they walked down the steep mountain road. They were entombed in the trees and the mountain, they were its prisoners until it decided to release them. They walked and they walked, following it's twisted path as it made its way to the town of Eden. It felt like the trees pity them as they passed through them, wondering why they were making such a foolish journey home, when it was clear that the town didn't want them anymore.

Arty Grape and Mr Fox held each other tight as they wandered and wondered when they would leave the dark forest. Strange sounds emanated from every part of the woods, animals seemed to roam free without a care in the world, squirrels jumped from tree to tree and looked at them apprehensively, wondering why they were roaming around their domain.

'Are you okay Arty?' asked Mr Fox.

'I'm okay. You okay?'

'I'm okay. How much further do you think it is?' wondered Mr Fox.

'I don't know. We've been walking for about an hour or more, I think we should be at the bottom soon.

As soon as Arty Grape finished her sentence the road started to level out and she saw an opening in the trees ahead; the light dashed forwards to greet them, they found themselves in the open air again. The trees and the darkness were behind them, but they were faced once again with a road that stretched in two directions and another dilemma to solve.

'It's this way.' pointed Arty Grape. 'I know where we are

now.' Arty Grape felt safer now that she knew where she was, so she took charge and guided her brother through the streets of Eden, even though Mr Fox knew where he was, he knew his sister wanted him to follow her. They passed several houses that they once knew, friends who resided at the factory on the hill were no longer there anymore. The houses looked abandoned as they stared at them, as they walked past them the more the houses revealed faint silhouettes of people standing behind the curtains, these strangers stood behind every window in every house along the way, looking back at them without being seen. The dark figures didn't move, they stood as still as they could, and every one of them stared at Arty Grape and Mr Fox as they passed by. They continued to walk through the empty streets of Eden, the town was desolate of any living soul, soon they arrived at the local shop which they knew would lead them to the last bend in the road before they would be able to see their house, a house which no longer felt like their home. Arty Grape and Mr Fox became nervous at exactly the same time, they could feel their stomachs tie into knots and their hearts sink in their chest. They didn't know what awaited them, but they had no choice but to find out. They slowly approached their home, their pace slowed with each step they took, eventually they came to a complete stop. They looked up to see the path that led them to house number zero and they stood still for a moment holding each other's hand. They dared not move, they dared not make a single sound for fear of disturbing whatever lay inside. They didn't know who or what to expect when they entered. Arty Grape started to slowly walk up the path, her legs carried her but she didn't know why. She reached the front door and slowly raised her arms and pushed it open with ease, gazing into the hallway, looking for any signs of life. The house seemed empty, devoid of any voices, televisions, radio or life. It felt eerie and strange but somewhat expected. Arty Grape pushed the door fully open and carefully walked in to the hallway, without thinking she began to make her way upstairs and Mr Fox followed closely behind her. They crept slowly upwards, their palms greased the bannister with their sweat as they moved, and the seventh step creaked as it usually did when they stepped on it, filling the world with the only sound. Step by step they made their way to their mama and papa's bedroom door and as they reached it Arty Grape didn't hesitate to push it carefully open. They walked slowly into their mama and papas bedroom hoping they would find them asleep or at least pretending to be asleep, as they usually did, instead they found them standing lifeless by the window. They looked at them, standing and staring out of the window before they turned around very slowly to greet them with huge smiles on their faces, it felt like they were elated to see them after all the time that had passed, it looked liked they were going to run towards them, pick them up, hug them and tell them how much they had missed them, express to them how sorry they had been for everything that had happened....and then the music began to play.

Jeepers creepers, where'd ya get those peepers?

Jeepers creepers, I'm coming for your eyes.

Blank Page

Why Are You Still Here. The Story Is Over, Go Home. Go And Do Something Else. I Know I Am........

Printed in Great Britain
by Amazon